Miracle
Wimp

Miracle
Wimp

by Erik P. Kraft

LITTLE, BROWN AND COMPANY

New York • Boston

Little, Brown and Company

Hachette Book Group USA
237 Park Avenue, New York, NY 10017
Visit our Web site at www.lb-teens.com

First Edition: August 2007

ISBN-13: 978-0-316-01165-5
ISBN-10: 0-316-01165-7

10 9 8 7 6 5 4 3 2 1

Q-FF

Book design by Tracy Shaw

Printed in the United States of America

The text was set in Bernhard Gothic, and the display type is Agency.

To the beautiful people.
There are a lot more of us than there are of you.

Miracle Wimp

MAYO, THOMAS

Miracle Wimp

In some ways, I guess I'm lucky. I'm not fat, so I miss out on all those good nicknames like "Moby," "Globe," and "Lardass." I don't have a lot of pimples, so I miss out on "Pizza Face" and "Goalie for the Dart Team." I'm average height, so no "Shrimpy" or any of that. I guess I should be thankful. However, my last name is Mayo, and I can't help but wonder if it were something different, would the Donkeys just ignore me? Maybe. But instead I'm Miracle Wimp. Pretty clever for a bunch of troglodytes. I've tried to explain to them on several occasions that Miracle Whip is not technically mayonnaise, it's actually "salad dressing" (read the label), but all I get is, "Yeah, whatever, Miracle Wimp," so I've given up trying.

Most of the time I get left alone. However, there are places where I am sometimes forced to mingle with my tormentors. For example: gym class. No getting out of this. My only hope would be to come down with some sort of affliction that would cause me to be wheelchair-bound between the hours of 7:50 AM and 2:10 PM, except for weekends and summers. But I've heard they've found a vaccine for whatever causes this, so I'm out of luck.

First Day of School

"So, what did you end up with for an elective?" Adam asked as we were walking down to the cafeteria.

"Wood Shop," I said. "I can't believe it. They totally screwed up my schedule."

"I somehow got chess. I don't even know how to play, but at least the people there aren't threatening. Awkward, perhaps. Threatening? Not at all."

"We totally should have started that Tiddlywinks elective last year. As the founders, we would've had to be in it."

"Yeah, but if they let us start our own, then everyone would have wanted to start one, and next thing you know, Steve's got Smoking third period."

"Well, at least he'd be getting class credit for it."

Not Chess

"Wait a minute," said Adam. "Wood Shop? With Mr. Boort?"

"Yeah," I said.

"You know about Mr. Boort, right?" he asked.

"Bad news," said Steve, who had just caught up to us.

"What are you talking about?" I asked.

"Bad news," said Steve.

"Not that crap about looking down girls' shirts," I said. "Half the teachers in this school would be working at McDonald's if you got fired for that. And that includes some of the ladies."

"No way," said Adam. "I heard that some kid threw a nail or a bolt or something at his head, and he got so pissed that he whacked the kid with a two-by-four and broke a bunch of his ribs. Or his arm. Or something."

"Bad news," said Steve.

"Is that all you have to offer?" I asked Steve.

"Well," said Steve, "I can tell you that Mr. Boort is very tall, he lives in a really bad part of Springfield, and he likes to chew on bouillon cubes."

"Still not very helpful, but better," I said.

Adam

Adam was a senior, but he was my best friend. I guess when the pickings are slim, you make friends with whoever. I suppose I could also look at it from the standpoint that I was so cool that a senior wanted to hang out with me, but whatever. He also had a girlfriend who was in college, so I guess he really spanned the age spectrum. It was just a community college and she lived at home with her parents, but college is college. He didn't really see her all that much, because college is a lot of work, but having a girlfriend who isn't around all that much is better than having no girlfriend.

Steve

I've known Steve since kindergarten. We were in the same class, and I noticed him because he drew people with square bodies. His handwriting is still very square.

Football

Fall, of course, means football. For the rougher set, there is the football team, or weekend games in the park. For the rest of us, who really don't care, there is gym, which is inescapable. At least we aren't allowed to tackle, which is out of the question for a lot of us anyway due to general feebleness. Instead, we get to wear these ridiculous belts with long ribbons hanging off them. This is "flag football" and these are the "flags," though that is a bit of a stretch of the term, I think. No soldiers ever went into battle waving such things, and certainly they were never saluted. In fact, they were held in place by duct tape, which really seemed a travesty. But this is hardly the worst part of it. Oh no. There are the "pinnies." I have never heard this word before, and I'm going to guess I never will again, once I never have to take gym again. Pinnies are these horrible fishnet jerseys one of the teams has to wear so we can tell one team from another. Not only are they fishnet, but they are bright orange, and have these elastic waistbands that ride up and make you look like some sort of orange netty mushroom. Compared to this, running around like an idiot grabbing at ribbons is downright dignified.

FOOT BALL

HERO

Drift

I'm not really sure why, but it seems like people don't stay friends forever. When you're little, everyone hangs out and it's no big deal. Then you get older and people get weird. Sometime around junior high school everyone starts deciding what's cool and what's not cool. As if this wasn't bad enough, in junior high they combine a couple of elementary schools, so all your old friends get split up. Then, once you've made your junior high friends, they split you up again in high school. And in high school, the cool vs. not cool thing is way worse.

This is not to say that you don't just sometimes stop being friends with people because they are jerks. But school bouncing everyone around sure doesn't help. Sometimes you lose good people, and sometimes you get crammed in there with some real prizewinners.

Sea of friends

SCHOOL

Steve Drift

Steve and I never really stopped being friends, we just fell victim to the constant shuffle. When we were in the same elementary school, we were in all the same classes. When we got to junior high, we weren't even on the same bus. I guess I'm just lazy, because that was really all it took for us to stop hanging out after elementary school. Every time we had to change schools there were new people, and maybe that made the old people seem less interesting.

Friends

Freshman year I had a couple of non-Steve and Adam friends. These guys Rob and Barry sat next to me in homeroom. They seemed like nice guys, and since we were all new to high school, I guess that's all it really took for us to become friends. Maybe that was too easy. Maybe I need to raise my standards.

Next year, I will choose friends from two rows over.

Screwed

I really wanted to take Computer Animation. I've tried to take Art before, but it's not considered an academic, and Mr. Banke, my guidance counselor, insists that I focus on college prep classes rather than wasting my time in Art. Animation was going to be the closest thing to Art I was going to get at this school. I really doubt I'll get to do much drawing in Shop.

FROM THE DESK OF

SHOP

Assignment 1:

Draw this Screw:

Guidance

"Mr. Banke, I think there's a problem with my schedule."

"Let me see." He put on his little half-glasses reading glasses. "Hmm. Mayo, Tom. Nope, you've got five classes, looks right to me."

"I've been put in Wood Shop. I in no way signed up for Wood Shop. It wasn't even an alternate. When I got my preliminary schedule at the end of last year, I had Computer Animation on there as an elective."

"Oh, well, that filled up quick."

"I know, I was in it."

"Well, there's nothing I can do about it now, the class is full. If you'd come to me at the end of last year, maybe I could have done something about it."

"Aren't you listening to me? I was in it at the end of last year. Something happened and my schedule got messed up."

He fiddled with some paper clips on his desk. "Well, sometimes things happen that are beyond our control. Maybe you were meant to take Wood Shop, and that's why this happened. Some things are just meant to be." He held up his hands in a "what are you gonna do?" sort of gesture.

"I assure you I am not meant to take Wood Shop."

"Well, it's out of my hands right now. Give it a shot—you might like it."

"I highly doubt that."

"A lot of the guys on the football team seem to like it."

"I'm dead," I mumbled to myself.

Animation

"How was it?" I asked Steve once he got back from what should have been my first animation class. He had somehow not gotten bumped. Lucky.

"It was okay. It was pretty full."

"Who else was in there?" I asked. Who took my spot?

"Well, me, obviously," said Steve. "Mary Clanningham, Robin the Slut, a bunch of people I don't remember. Bunch of idiots, really."

"So do any of those people even have an interest in this stuff?"

"Beats me," said Steve. "They probably signed up thinking they were going to watch cartoons instead of make them."

"Or maybe they got randomly assigned like I did. Mr. Banke probably screwed something up on the computer because he doesn't know what he's doing."

"Heh," said Steve. "You can Banke on that! Obviously he has no idea what he's doing. Why else would he become a guidance counselor at the school he went to?"

"Seriously?"

"Yeah, he went off to college, then came back and settled in."

"Great. And he's helping us plan our futures. We're doomed."

"Well, at least he left for a while. Bob the Janitor graduated and then started right in as a janitor. All the teachers were kind of like, 'What are you still doing here?' I don't know if Mr. Banke was involved in that career choice or not, but it wouldn't surprise me."

"Maybe he was meant to be a janitor," I said. "Mr. Banke can tap into the cosmos."

"So, how was Shop?" he asked.

The Mr. Boort Volunteer Fire Department

"Mr. Boort, I think the sander's on fire."

"What are you talking about, you bananahead?"

"There's smoke coming out of the belt sander."

Mr. Boort gave a short grunt, scrunched up his eyebrows, and after a minute or so of what may have been contemplation, grabbed his cup of coffee and slowly walked out into the main workshop area where we all stood, our projects abandoned on the workbenches, staring at the smoke.

Mr. Boort walked up to the machine and sniffed at it. He circled the machine, trying to peer down into various holes. He got back to the front of the machine, where the biggest gap was—between the sandpaper and the platform the wood rested on while you sanded it—leaned forward and peered down into this hole, stood back up straight, snorted, and then dumped his coffee down the hole.

"Better keep an eye on that," he said as he yanked the plug out of the wall by the cord. "Now get back to work!"

Mr. Boort, Art Critic

Mr. Boort runs his class in an unusual fashion. Me and Jimmy Buncho were making assignment #1: magazine racks with little hearts sawed into the sides of the base. Mine looked o.k., but Jimmy really wasn't putting his, well, heart into his. Mr. Boort came by to see how things were coming along. He picked up mine, looked it over, grunted a beef-flavored grunt, and put it down. He walked over to Jimmy's, picked it up, looked at it from all sides, and announced, "This thing shits," and tossed it in the trash.

Bolos

"Are you a bolo or not a bolo?" Mr. Boort likes to ask. I have been deemed a non-bolo. I don't know what I did to achieve non-bolo status, but one day I walked up to Mr. Boort and said, "Mr. Boort, may I use the router?" and Mr. Boort looked me up and down for a minute and then said, "Sure, you don't look like a bolo."

Mr. Boort also likes to call people peanutheads. I think being a peanuthead is better than being a bolo, but not by much. It may be the final step in the evolution of a bolo.

Thankfully, I am not a peanuthead either.

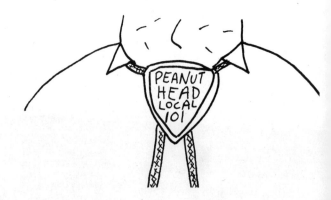

Funny

Apparently I'm kind of funny, but people hardly ever notice because they don't normally pay any attention to me. Or if they do, it's the wrong kind of attention, and they're not going to hear what I have to say because they're too focused on roughing me up.

Do girls like funny? They don't pay attention to me either. Even if I knew how to approach them, I'd never get past my first sentence before they'd walk away or shut me down. All this comedy gold is going to waste.

Psych

One day last year as class was letting out, my Psychology teacher asked me to stay after class. "Why are you in this class?" she asked me.

"I just thought it was interesting," I said. It was generally known that this was an easy class, but I thought that the subject matter was pretty interesting, and not a lot of schools offered it. I thought I could get out of it what I put into it.

"Well, you're doing too well," she said. "With the curve, you have well over a one hundred average, and some of the other students have begun cheating off you. They went from failing every test, to getting nineties on the last one. I'm going to have to move your desk."

THEY STEAL MY BRAINS!

"Why do I have to move? I'm not the one cheating."

"Yes, but you're also not going to 'act out' as a result of this," she said.

Apparently even teachers think I'm a wimp.

Drawing

When I get stressed out, I like to draw to try to feel better.

I get stressed out a lot. School can be kind of awful.

Everything can be kind of awful, actually.

If I can draw a comic about it, I feel a little better. Sometimes I don't even have to do a whole comic. Once I was at the doctor's office and there was this lady sitting across from me in the waiting room who had the nastiest teeth I'd ever seen. They were big, they stuck out, and they were the color green I had only seen in ugly sweaters before. It made me really sad. I mean, what's it like to go through life when you look like that?

So I took out my notebook and pretended to be writing down some really important stuff, but I was actually drawing her. And when I was done, I somehow felt better. You'd think I'd want to forget someone who made me feel bad, but it didn't really work that way.

Meant to Be

Who determines what is or isn't meant to be anyway? Obviously Mr. Banke was lazy and didn't feel like correcting his mistakes. Is this how fate always gets determined? Something goes wrong in the cosmic computer, but the Great Guidance Counselor just doesn't feel like fixing it, so you're stuck?

So maybe I'm supposed to be the biggest babe magnet in this school, but the Great Guidance Counselor hit the wrong key while entering stuff in one day, but fixing it meant turning the computer back on and hitting a couple of keys, so forget it.

Home Ec

Not too many girls take Shop. They mostly take Home Economics. For them it's the lesser of two evils. Home Ec is bad, but at least there's no Mr. Boort who may or may not be looking down their shirts. Their teacher is just as weird as Mr. Boort, but the weirdness manifests itself in a less menacing manner. She just seems high, where Mr. Boort seems to commute from Neptune every morning. And high people generally don't go around breaking people's ribs.

The few girls who do take Wood Shop are troll-like and dangerous. They smell like ashtrays, have hair bigger than my body, and they squawk a lot. They also aren't very coordinated. Regina Ferrigno once maimed my hand. We were making these awful duck marionettes, and to get the rope that was their legs to stay in the leg holes in the body, you had to melt the ends of the rope with a lighter and then stick them into the holes while they were still molten. Rather than blowing the flaming rope out with her mouth, as Mr. Boort had instructed us to do, she waved the rope around in the air, which is how it came to smack into my hand, where it did go out. I held my hand out and yelled, and then for some reason she dropped the hot metal lighter into my outstretched palm. I threw it at her, but I was in so much pain I didn't really get up the force I was hoping for.

Mr. Boort came over, saw what had happened, called her a bolohead (the worst!) and ran my hand under cold water in a nearby sink. This only served to make the waxy stuff on the rope harden, so it took off more skin when we peeled it off. Since she had proven herself a bolohead, Regina was denied the use of fire in Shop after that.

Mr. Boort's Hat

For a while, Mr. Boort wore this little yellow wool hat all the time. "Where'd you get that hat, Mr. Boort?" someone once yelled during attendance.

"He was fast, but I was faster," Mr. Boort mumbled with a big grin on his face, never looking up from the attendance sheet.

The Nerd Hierarchy

Hot Pink!

Even the low end of the food chain needs to establish a pecking order. In shop it was pretty easy. We nerds could have banded together and formed a support group for victims of the Donkeys, but it felt much better to pass along all the abuse we got. Robert Manly was our low man of choice.

1) He was new.
2) He wore pink sweatpants in gym class.
3) When made fun of by everyone about the sweatpants, his defense was: "They're my mother's!" That was too much for anybody.

Since none of us were big enough to actually beat on one another and do any real damage, we needed implements of destruction to do battle with. Fortunately we were surrounded by wood and tools, so fashioning such devices was no problem. The weapon of choice was the wooden Chinese throwing star. It was easily concealed, would hurt you even if it was thrown by a wimp, and could be made out of the smallest scraps of wood you could find.

All we needed was for Robert to get to a spot where we could get a clear shot at him without the risk of hitting someone bigger than us by accident. We didn't even actually have to hit him. The first shot only needed to get close enough to him for him to take cover. Once he did, we could keep him trapped for the whole period. Any time he stuck his head out, one of us would throw another star at him and he'd stay put for a few more minutes. He didn't dare retaliate for fear of missing us and hitting one of the Donkeys, and Mr. Boort was too busy eating bouillon cubes in his office to notice any atrocities taking place in the workshop.

When we ceased fire and lined up for the bell, we were all subject to wedgies given out by the Donkeys. It didn't matter that we had proven ourselves to be predators, or that Robert had already taken quite a bit of abuse that period. We all just had to stand with our backs to the wall, and hope the bell rang early.

Band

I'm not sure exactly, but I think I'm better off than if I was in Band. On the one hand, Band kids have their own sort of built-in group of friends just by being in Band. On the other hand, their group of friends is really, really dorky. They act like they're cool, and they get to hang out in the Band Room, but no one wants to hang out in the Band Room but Band kids. Possibly because it's full of Band kids.

They wear Band jackets like it's a sports team. The thing is, if you've got a football or wrestling team jacket on, people might think twice about messing with you. If you've got a Band jacket on, they might think twice about NOT messing with you.

I guess not everyone in Band is awful, but the awful ones are the ones you notice. I'm not exactly sure why they think they are so cool. School Band is way different from being in real band. Unless their real band is a smooth jazz band. That would be close in terms of uncoolness.

Speaking of Smooth Jazz

We did have a jazz band in our school. They weren't smooth jazz, but they were close. The kids in Band who were really good at their instruments got to be in Jazz Band, which made them think they were really elite. Which made them that much more unbearable. They even got the name changed from "Jazz Band" to "Synovia." One of them was in AP Biology, and learned that synovial fluid is what keeps your joints from wearing down. So, in a sense, I guess their name is smooth, even if their jazz isn't.

Cooler Than Not Cool

I'm not sure which is worse. Being not cool, or being not cool and acting like you are extremely cool. Who do people think they're trying to kid? Do they think that if they act cool for long enough, people will forget they're not cool?

Sorry, friend, that's not how it works. The cool people never forget. And the rest of us aren't going to let you off that easily.

Rob and Barry

Rob and Barry liked making videos when we were outside of school, which I thought was pretty cool. Mainly we'd just make stuff up as we went along, using whatever toys Rob's little brother and sister left lying around. There were a lot of videos of army guys saying lewd things to Barbies. Then we'd have to tape over them in case Rob's mother found them. You'd think she'd get suspicious of why there were so many videos of the wall or the carpet with the soundtrack of us in the other room getting food. Maybe she'd think it was art or something.

Flair

Despite my last name, I'm not really into condiments. Often this gets me weird looks from serving types, but what are you going to do? I also get bored just asking for "plain whatever on white," so every once in a while I try to mix it up.

There was this one lunch lady who always seemed to be in a bad mood, so one day I thought I could brighten her day with a new ordering style.

"Turkey, straight-up on white, please," I said.

She stared at me for a minute like I was possibly the biggest jackass to have ever ordered a turkey sandwich. "You mean plain turkey on white bread."

"I like to have a little flair," I said.

She made the sandwich and rolled her eyes at me as she handed it over. If there's one thing I can't stand, it's when people roll their eyes at me. So much for my good deed for the day.

As I was walking away, I heard Adam place his order. "Give me a roast beef," he said, "and make it sing."

Atomic Wedgies

Regular underpants remain in 1 piece, causing wedgie pain

One day, Matt Trumbull and Mike Stankiewicz, two of the lead Donkeys and the most active of our tormentors, were too busy punching each other to notice the kids up against the wall. Then, without warning, Ken Windell, who usually only directed his aggression towards the other Donkeys, saw an opportunity he obviously couldn't pass up. Rob Johnson had leaned away from the wall ever so slightly, and Ken just had to go for it. He yanked as hard as he could, and was able to lift Rob off the ground by his underpants to the point where he was hanging horizontally. His screams for mercy went unheard. While this distracted us, a full wedgie attack was launched. I felt a hand go down the back of my pants, and someone yelled "Miracle wedgie!" I tried to run, but I wasn't fast enough. I braced for the pain that was sure to follow, but all I felt was a tug, and then I heard a ripping sound. "Whoa, even his underwear's wimpy," I heard Matt say, and then I was free.

Silently, I thanked my mother for buying me crummy Kmart underwear.

Cheap underpants unique, flyaway waistband provides testicular safety

Bikini Briefs?

Could bikini briefs be the answer to Atomic Wedgies? Yes or no? That was a question I had long grappled with. They were small enough that they might be unreachable in the event of a wedgie attack. The downside was, they'd probably cause excruciating pain if a wedgie was successful, due to the lack of breathing room. It seemed (based on my inspections in the stores) that they were made of more durable material than tighty-whities, which meant my hopes of being saved by a low-quality waistband again were probably nonexistent.

Of course, I had overlooked the whole "colored underpants" aspect of bikini briefs, and unfortunately had to realize it in gym class. I was busy changing, and then I heard someone yell out, "Underoos!" But they at least didn't try to yank on my Underoos, so for the time being I was unharmed.

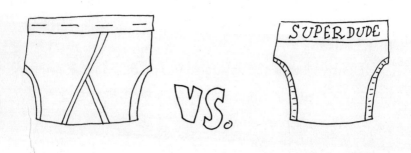

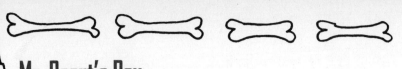

Mr. Boort's Box

I went into Mr. Boort's office to ask him a question about whether I could paint my project instead of staining it. It was covered in pencil marks because I had done a really crappy job of measuring it, and this would be obvious if I didn't completely cover it up. He had his back to the door and seemed kind of surprised when I walked in.

"What?" he said. And then he started to put something in his desk drawer.

"What's that?" I asked without thinking. It's probably a bad idea to pry when you're dealing with a dangerous individual like Mr. Boort, but too late.

"It's just something I made a long time ago," he said, and handed it to me. It was a wooden box about the size of a shoebox, but it had a dragon carved on the top, and all along the edges he had carved little skulls and bones.

"I did that when I got back from the service," he said. "I guess I was in kind of a morbid mood."

"Did you carve all this?"

"All by hand. I didn't have much work at the time. Had to do something."

He had done a really nice job of it, but it was just so strange.

"So why are you bothering me?"

Not So Animated

"Well, as it turns out," Steve said, "you're not missing much by not having Animation."

"What do you mean?"

"Well, Mr. Curnty doesn't really know what he's doing, both computer-wise and running a class-wise. On the bright side, we get pizza or donuts every class."

"Huh?"

"Well, class is either first thing in the morning or during lunch period. 'Mr. Curnty, we're getting donuts,' or 'Mr. Curnty, we're getting a pizza,' is all it takes, if we share with him. I mean, it's kind of cool, but I haven't really learned anything. But I'm one of the few people in there that actually wanted to be in there."

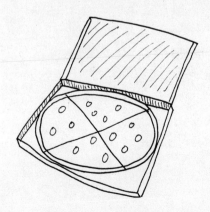

"Cool"

Back in junior high, I made an attempt to "fit in." I thought that was what you were supposed to do. It was a new school, and I wasn't really sure of how to make new friends. Going up and talking to people wasn't cutting it. You'd think walking up to someone you didn't know and saying "hi," would be a good first step, but this wasn't the experience I had. Somehow they could tell that I wasn't "cool" or whatever they thought "cool" was. They were so good at telling I wasn't cool that *they didn't even have to speak to me to figure it out.* No interview session, no trial period. Apparently my "hi" gave me away. Something in my voice? Should I have said "what's up?" I don't know.

Pants

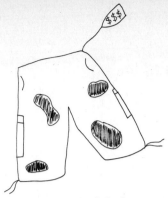

I decided I would break into the group of kids everyone thought was cool. No one seemed to be able to explain to me what made them cool, though. Sort of like how I was just uncool. I should have realized that something like this was possibly meddling with forces bigger than I was, but my thinking was obviously muddled.

The cool kids all seemed to wear these giant army pants. They were kind of ridiculous, very puffy, and had lots of pockets all over the place. They weren't real army pants, either. They were really expensive pants that looked like camouflage army pants. It didn't make sense to me, but maybe that was due to my uncoolness. Once I had the pants, I figured I'd understand. Pants bring knowledge.

Cheaping Out

The problem with The Pants (besides the ridiculousness of how they looked) was the expensiveness of the "real" ones. My parents were not going to pay for those pants. I had some money from mowing lawns, but it wasn't enough for The Pants. So I figured I could go and buy regular army pants, but get them too big so they'd be baggy enough. I saved $60, and they were basically the same thing. I was convinced I had broken into coolness at a fraction of the cost.

Geeking Out

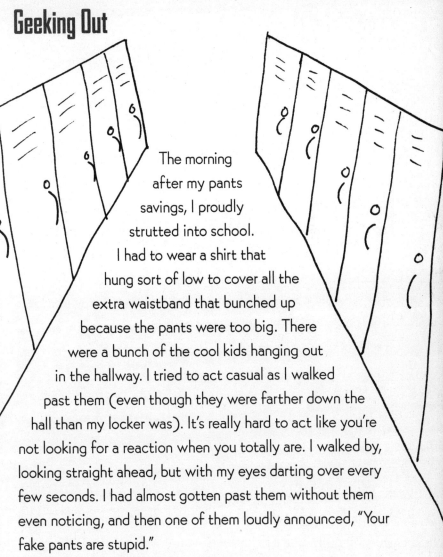

The morning after my pants savings, I proudly strutted into school. I had to wear a shirt that hung sort of low to cover all the extra waistband that bunched up because the pants were too big. There were a bunch of the cool kids hanging out in the hallway. I tried to act casual as I walked past them (even though they were farther down the hall than my locker was). It's really hard to act like you're not looking for a reaction when you totally are. I walked by, looking straight ahead, but with my eyes darting over every few seconds. I had almost gotten past them without them even noticing, and then one of them loudly announced, "Your fake pants are stupid."

Then there were a lot of giggles.

Then I had to walk past them again to go to my locker.

Freaking Out

To make matters worse, I had a run-in with these awful little kids on my way home from school that day. I'd see them a lot if I walked home a certain way. It was much shorter to go down the street their house was on, but some days I had other stuff to do so I'd go a different way.

Anyway, these kids sucked. They were always up to something. Throwing rocks at bee's nests. Throwing rocks at dogs. Throwing rocks at cars. They had these awful rat-tail haircuts too. I always wondered what kind of parent would give their kid a rat-tail hair cut.

Apparently it's the same kind of parent that thinks it's a good idea to let their smart-ass little kids play with a paintball gun. Because that's what they had. I turned the corner onto their street and saw what was going on, but they also saw me turn onto the street. If I had turned back and gone a different way, they totally would have chased me down. I kind of had to meet them head-on if I was going to get by.

"Nice army pants, army man," the one with the gun said. He seemed to be the oldest. All three of them had dirt mous-taches. I had never gotten close enough to them to notice this before.

"Do you want to play army with us, army man?" he asked in a really snotty tone.

"Uh, not really," I said.

"Then why are you wearing army pants, army man?"

"It's complicated," I said.

He stared at me for a minute.

"I don't like you, army man," he said.

Have you ever been shot in the balls with a paintball gun up close?

Well, I have. It's not something I'd like to have happen again.

By the time I had gotten home, a bunch of the paint had dried, and it wouldn't come out in the wash, so there was no way I could return those stupid pants.

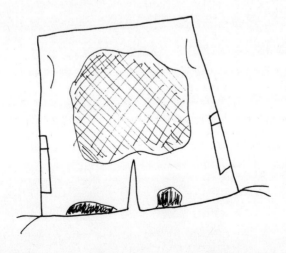

It Is Decided

Once the pain subsided and I was able to think clearly again, I came to the decision that maybe it wasn't worth being cool if it was expensive, humiliating, and resulted in severe testicular distress. It seemed pretty obvious to me that I didn't have "it," and since I couldn't even recognize what "it" was, I was probably never going to get "it."

I also decided I really didn't want to hang out with people who thought it was cool to say "your fake pants are stupid" to strangers.

Not Much to Do

We didn't really have that much to do in our town. Obviously we weren't going to go to parties. If we didn't like the people anyway, they certainly don't get any better when they've been drinking. Adam could get his parents' car whenever he wanted, so we drove around a lot. There were lots of farmy areas and empty woodsy streets not too far from our town, and we spent a good portion of our time driving around these. At least there was no one out there to bother us.

But a lot of times we'd just end up at someone's house watching TV.

Adam's Girlfriend

Once in a while we'd end up at Adam's girlfriend's house. Her parents never seemed to be around. She lived on one of those out-in-the-middle-of-nowhere streets. Sure, we usually just ended up watching TV there too, but it seemed more exotic because it wasn't Adam's or Steve's house.

Her name was Becky Frunecki. That totally sucks.

How the Fruneckis spent their honeymoon

Some Weekends

Some weekends Adam would go off with Becky, usually if she was caught up with her schoolwork, or just blowing it off. Since Adam was our ride, that killed it for me and Steve. I don't know what Steve would do, but I'd sometimes end up reading, or maybe just going to bed early.

I don't know why sometimes it was o.k. for us to hang out with Adam and Becky, and sometimes it wasn't. Well, actually, I guess I do.

Meet Larry

Larry was this guy at our school who was in the Special Ed. class, but he used to eat lunch with everyone else. We got to know him because he was looking for a place to sit, and Rob, my new friend from homeroom, was wearing a Red Sox shirt, which apparently made for a good ice-breaker.

"You like the Red Sox?" Larry said, sitting down.

"I'm wearing the shirt," said Rob.

"My dad and I sometimes go to Red Sox games. They don't always win."

"No shit," said Rob.

"I'm Larry," said Larry.

"Good for you," said Rob.

"I'm Tom," I said. I didn't know why Rob was being such a jerk. Larry hadn't done anything, he just wanted somewhere to sit.

"What are people going to think when they see us sitting with that retard?" was Rob's answer when I asked him later.

Driver's License

One of the few things as terrible as having to take Shop is not having my license. The buses around here are few and far between, and they don't really go many places. Maybe to the bus station, but that's kind of it, unless you live downtown. They'll cart you around the downtown area, but escape is difficult. The schedule says buses come infrequently, and reality says it's even less than that. If you want to get anywhere good, you need your license. I'll be getting mine soon, and maybe then I can get out of my house once in a while and seek adventure.

Can't Have One Without the Other

I'm assuming that getting a girlfriend will go along with getting my license. As though license trumps nerd. Some sort of nerd antidote, if you will.

Sometimes my father tells me I have to learn how the world works. I'm worried that this might be the type of thing he's talking about.

Mary Clanningham

Sometimes people can overcome their inherent suckiness and be kind of nice. Take, for example, Mary Clanningham. When we first met in elementary school, I thought she was the devil because she would run around trying to kiss all the boys at recess. Oddly enough, at the time this was considered uncool. Once she outgrew that phase we got along, because everyone pretty much gets along in elementary school, unless you smell or have cooties or something. But the thing about Mary is, once we got to junior high and the Donkeys and the nerds developed, she never stopped being nice to me. It was like we never left elementary school. She was one of the most popular and definitely one of the best-looking people in school, but she always said hi and would talk to me if we had a class together. Maybe she was dropped as a baby and it destroyed the part of her brain that made coolness distinctions. But I always respected her for that, once I was done admiring her beauty. It makes me feel bad that I used to call her "Mary-fairy crammin' ham" when we were little.

Oh, and another thing about her that's kind of impor-

tant is that her shirts always matched her socks. Always.
Pretty snazzy.

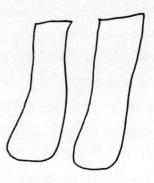

Larry Feels the Heat

The first month or so of school you always get a few pretty hot days. Shorts aren't allowed (except in gym), so that makes it all the more unbearable. Sometimes they'd open the emergency exit doors of the cafeteria to try to air out the heat from the kitchen, but that really didn't do much. Hot air that moves around is still hot air.

I was sitting with Rob and Barry, and we were all sweating profusely. Larry came bouncing into the cafeteria. He had really bad pit stains, but it didn't seem to faze him at all. He actually never seemed anything but happy, which I guess is kind of admirable, at least given how miserable I feel all the time.

"Ugh, here comes Larry," said Rob.

"Hot enough for you guys?" said Larry.

"Shut up, Larry," said Rob.

"No, Larry, turn up the heat some more," said Barry.

"You guys are funny," said Larry, not even noticing the hate.

Rob and Barry didn't say anything for the rest of the time Larry was there. They wouldn't even look at him.

"It's sure hot," Larry would say every once in a while.

From then on Rob and Barry would say "Hot enough for you guys?" whenever one of them thought the other had done something stupid.

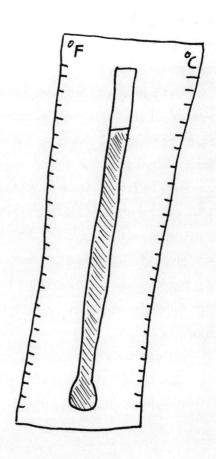

Heads

Aside from the Donkeys, another potential threat to the well-being of a wimp is the Heads. These are the kids who seem to come to school just to cause trouble. They smoke, act up in class, if they even go at all, and wear the same heavy metal T-shirts every day and didn't seem to care that everyone noticed.

I get along well with most of the Heads. I've taken gym with all of them at one time or another, since most of them seem to take gym four times a day. But even though they take it so much, they never seem to have their gym stuff. So they fail, even though you can get a C just by having your stuff and showing up.

The Heads like me because I make them laugh and I'm not afraid to make fun of them. I figure if they get mad at me I can probably outrun them since they are smokers. Like one time this big guy, Cosimo, was wearing these pointy cowboy boots. I asked him, "Are those pointy so you can still get the cockroaches when they run into the corner?"

Man, by the way Cosimo laughed, you'd have thought I'd said something really funny.

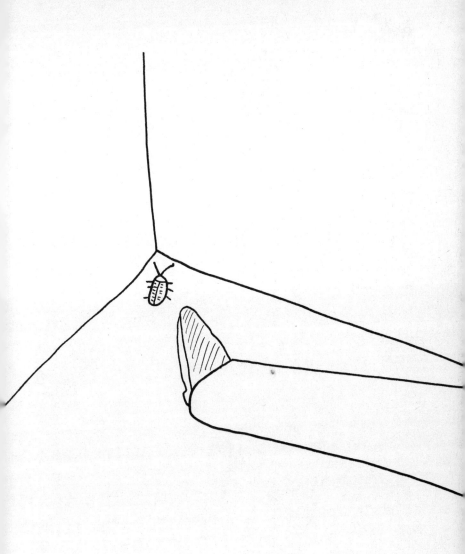

Spaceships

One thing Cosimo didn't laugh at was when people walked up behind him and said, "We are the voyagers on the spaceship Cosimo. . . ."

I mean, I thought it was funny when other people did it, but I *totally* played it cool.

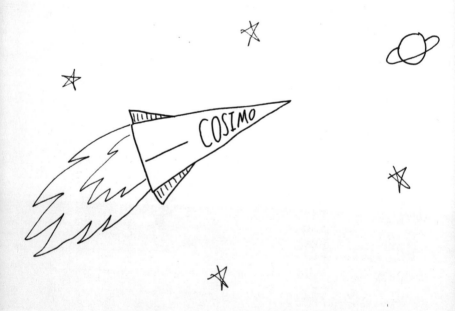

Wimp

What exactly is a wimp, anyway? Well, I suppose if it's the opposite of being a Donkey, I'm definitely there. I'm not a Head, and Heads are in some ways just the substance-abuse angle of the Donkeys taken to the extreme. Sure, fine, I'm a nerd. I don't care. I don't see anything wrong with that. I'm not about to go and beat on people because they don't use their brains, but I suppose that makes me a wimp. Those different from you need beatings, not understanding. Also, the complete lack of muscle tone doesn't help my case much.

Someday none of this will matter.

Right?

MARCH 2237

		1 it matters	2 it matters	3 it matters	4 it matters	5 it matters	6 it matters
7 it matters	8 it matters	9 it matters	10 it matters	11 it matters	12 it matters	13 it matters	
14 it matters	15 it matters	16 it matters	17 it matters	18 it matters	19 it matters	20 it matters	
21 it matters	22 it matters	23 it matters	24 it matters	25 it matters	26 it matters	27 it matters	
28 it matters	29 no longer matters!	30 oh crap. It matters again.	31 you're long dead anyway				

The In-Crowd

DRUNKEN COOKOUT "IN CROWD" Welcome   VS.   STREET FAIR Hot enough for you?

This one Saturday there was going to be this artsy street fair downtown that some "weird" bands were going to play at. It sounded like fun to me, or at least more interesting than doing nothing at all. Rob and Barry weren't into it. All they wanted to do was go to some drunken cookout at some upperclassman's house. We probably could have done both, but neither side was going to give. "Ooh yeah, street fair," Rob said. "Hot enough for you guys?"

I walked into the kitchen because I was really annoyed, but I also wanted something to drink. Rob's mother was in there doing the dishes. "So, what are you guys up to this afternoon?" she asked.

"Well, I want to go to this street fair that's going on downtown," I said.

"Oh, is that what the 'in-crowd' is doing today?"

"Uh, I really don't think so," I said.

I stood there silently, and then, forgetting why I had gone into the kitchen, I walked back into the living room where Barry and Rob were.

The "in-crowd." Who actually says that?

The Secret Knock

The most important thing you can ever know is that you always—always—knock first and say "it's cool" before you go into the bathroom by the office. Despite its proximity to the Den of All Power (DOAP), this is the bathroom that everyone smokes in. I probably don't need to say why you need to say "it's cool." If you don't say it, all the smokers will throw their cigarettes in the toilets when they hear the door open. You'd get a serious ass-kicking if they throw their cigarettes out prematurely. Most of us used other bathrooms just in case we momentarily forgot to use the secret knock. Sometimes the mind wanders. But I'd occasionally go in there to look for Steve. I knew a few non-Heads who smoked, but Steve was the only one who smoked in the Heads' bathroom. That was right up there with parking in the back of the parking lot. Steve didn't have a car, so I guess this was how he tried to show he was tough. I don't think anyone was convinced.

Steve smoked "light" cigarettes. This amused the Heads to no end. I think that had a lot to do with them allowing Steve to smoke in their bathroom. Steve was accepted because he smoked and observed the secret knock, and when he was in there the Heads would make fun of him for smoking lights and he took it well.

I asked Steve once why the vice principal never tried to use the secret knock to bust people.

"Are you kidding?" Steve asked, laughing so hard he blew smoke out his nose. "Can you see Hammo dressed up in his Head outfit trying to blend in?" He was still laughing, but started talking in a stiff-sounding voice. "Robert G. Hammo approaching. It is cool." He tried to take another drag on his cigarette, but wouldn't stop laughing for another few minutes.

MEN

Library

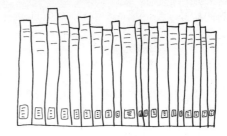

I like the library because it's quiet and they have a lot of books, which I enjoy. It's also a good place for me to sit and draw. The bad thing about the library is that if you go there at night, it's sometimes full of Donkeys. There's no way to really know if it is or not either, unless you happen to know when every test for every class is. Usually they go to the library the night before a test and figure out ways to cheat. Anyway, you have to walk past all the study tables to get to the book return, checkout table, and catalogs, and really, the chances of me walking through there and NOT getting harassed are pretty slim, so I pretty much avoid the library after five.

Let's Go to Work

The best thing about Shop is attendance. Not because I enjoy being counted, or sitting in a room with the rest of the degenerates that take Shop, but because when we're done being counted, Mr. Boort always yells, "Let's go to work!" and we all get up and run out into the workshop area, and for a second we're all inspired and in love with life. Then we realize that we're making magazine racks with little hearts in the base, and we're jarred back to reality. If only there was a way to feel like Mr. Boort had just yelled "Let's go to work!" all the time.

A lot of stuff goes on prior to attendance. Sometimes Mr. Boort takes ten minutes in his office before he comes into the attendance room. This is usually the time to catch up on gossip or get into "shenanigans." One time the Donkeys forced this kid Rob Stein into a cabinet in the attendance room and jammed a big file through the door handles so he couldn't get out. When Mr. Boort finally arrived to take attendance, he looked around and yelled, "Where's Stein?" Somebody pointed over to the cabinet. Mr. Boort wandered over to the cabinet mumbling something about peanutheads. He pulled out the file and opened the doors. "You Stein?" he asked.

"Yeah," said Rob.

"All right then," Mr. Boort said, and he shut the doors and jammed the file back in the handles. "Let's go to work!"

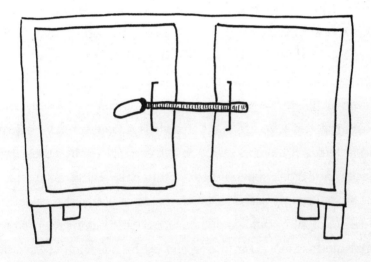

Derondo's

Have you ever noticed a place in your town that always seems to be something different? I mean a store that's a new store every time you go by it? In our town we had a pizza place that was a different pizza place every time. Well, at least for a while. I only knew it as two pizza places, but I've been told that it was at least five others before it was Diana's. We started going there in seventh grade on half days from school. Then in eighth grade it became Derondo's. It was more or less the same place. They didn't change the furniture or anything, maybe just the sign. And I think the sauce on the pizza got a little sweeter, but I'm not sure. But we still hung out there anyway. Then in ninth grade it moved from one end of the building it was in to the other. The building had like five shops in it, three of which never changed, one that changed all the time, and then the one that had just changed. So Derondo's moved down to the other end to a bigger spot and has been doing fine. The spot it used to be in then became a Laundromat, then a hair place, and now I think it's a place that sells fancy faucets. But anyway, Derondo's is a place we like to go with each other because there's always other kids there and you can check out the cute girls. It's not a place you want to go with your parents, because you feel dorky having your parents around when you're around other kids, and if they catch you looking at girls they're bound to make some sort of comment to embarrass you. Parents would never have gone to Derondo's in the spot it used to be in. It was too small and dumpy inside. I guess it was supposed to be more of a takeout place, except for teenagers. Maybe they expanded to get more of the parent market. Or maybe they knew that if they stayed in the other spot they'd go out of business in a matter of time and fled the first chance they got.

Oh, and I once found $20 in their parking lot.

Going Out

When you want to "go out" with someone, are you supposed to ask, "Do you want to go out with me?"

I never understood that. Once in fifth grade I liked this girl Lori and she liked me. That made sense. Then someone said to me, "Oh, so you're going out?"

"I don't think so," I said.

"But you both like each other and told each other so."

"Yes."

"Then you're going out."

"But we only see each other in school, we never actually 'go out.'"

"That doesn't matter. You're still going out with her."

"I don't think so."

"Yes, you are. That's just what it's called."

"Why do they call it that?"

"Because that's what it's called."

Things I Know About Dating at This Point

You must never *ever* say you don't know if your parents will let you go out with someone.

Ever.

I can say with much confidence that this is an extremely bad move because I've done it myself. I don't know why I said it, it just came out. Nerves are evil.

I was in seventh grade at the time and had taken a liking to an eighth grader, which was ambitious for a popular seventh grader, and totally ridiculous for someone of my social rank.

However, as luck would have it one day, this girl and her friends happened to be eating at what was Diana's at the time on the same half day as my friends and I. And her friends knew that I liked her and took it upon themselves to force her into our booth and pull my arm around her. She smelled like baby powder and it hung in the air even after she had wriggled away from me and out of the booth. One of her friends sat down in her place.

"You like Heidi, right?"

"Yeah."

"So, do you want to go out with her?"

Here's where I said it.

Choking back laughter, her friend ran outside to get her and dragged her back in and repeated the forcing of her into the booth, but she squirmed out again. This time as she made for the door her friend yelled out, "But don't you want to go out with him?"

"I don't know if I can," she managed to force out behind barely stifled laughter.

"I wanted to kick you when you said that," one of my friends told me after lunch.

"Well, it would have been too late anyway," I said as I felt myself falling into a deep funk, knowing that my already slim chances of going out with her had just turned anorexic and died.

PERMISSION SLIP

Tom Mayo has Permission To go out with the ladies.

his Mom
signature

More Problems with Dating

Inevitably, if the person you like is worth liking at all, a few other people also like them. Now, these other people may or may not know that you also like the person they like, but if they do, you'd better hope that they like competition. If not, you could find yourself in some pretty hairy situations.

For example, in my ill-fated attempts to woo the fair Heidi in Diana's that day, I managed to run afoul of the disagreeable John Chevrin. Heidi didn't want anything to do with him either, as he was just a little too much of a degenerate to be attractive. But he didn't care, and he surely didn't like competition. I know this because shortly after Heidi fled my floundering advances of sorts, the man-child John dumped a bunch of sugar in my hair from the booth behind me. My request for him to cut it out only resulted in his repeatedly asking me, "You wanna make something of it?"

I didn't, so I got up to leave. He followed me to the parking lot, and proceeded to show me how good he was at pushing. Finally, the novelty must have worn off because he stopped.

Sometimes, these ill-wishers assume a less obvious role.

Earlier in my high school career I was fascinated by Jen Maine, who was a year younger than me, but much, much cooler. A "friend" of mine (well, he sat next to me in English, and I'd explain to him what everything we read meant) moved in some of the cooler circles. I asked him to feel her out and find out if she knew who I was, and if there was even the remotest chance of our getting together, or if he'd orchestrate some activity in which we'd both be present. He kept saying he would, but always found some reason to not have done so: forgetting, too many people around, she was in a bad mood, etc. I kept pressing him and finally one day he just blurted out, "Look, I like her too, okay?" That was the end of that line of questioning. And of his passing English.

The Telephone

I kind of hate talking on the telephone. I don't know why that is, really. I guess maybe I feel weird about talking to someone I can't see. If it's someone I know, it's o.k., because I can sort of picture them, but it's still freaky. If it's someone I don't know, it really freaks me out. If it's someone I've only met once or twice, I sometimes have trouble visualizing the person, as they may not be fresh in my memory. This usually keeps me from paying attention to the conversation, which makes it worse.

So anyway, phones—I don't like them. I imagine I will need to get over this if and when I get a girlfriend. Rumor has it that girls like to talk on the phone.

Boobs and Butt

One of the things the Donkeys liked to do was piss off Mr. Boort by asking him annoying questions. It was really hard to piss Mr. Boort off for some reason, so the questions got worse as time went on. One of their favorite things to ask him about was Lyman Street, the street in Springfield where all the prostitutes hang out. They liked to ask him these things during attendance time, since there was a good audience then.

"Hey, Mr. Boort, you been down to Lyman Street lately?" is one of their favorites.

Some of Mr. Boort's answers:

1) "Yeah, I went down there the other night and got me some boobs and butt." (He's only said this once, and it's hotly debated whether or not he actually said it. I was there so I can assure you this is legitimate.)
2) "No, I don't get to see your friends much anymore." (Not as exciting as #1, but somehow appropriate given the maturity level of who he's dealing with.)
3) "Shut up, you bananaheads." (A far too frequent response.)

I sometimes wondered if the Donkeys even knew where Lyman Street was.

Skanks

There sure are a lot of skanks in my school. You know, girls who will do anything with anyone. Or almost anyone. I don't know that they'd do anything with me, and I don't really want to know. I find the whole idea revolting. I suppose if you're the type of person who just wants to have sex with someone, maybe this is your scene. But I don't see the point. It seems like there is so much in the world that doesn't mean anything, why add one more thing? Especially when you have the chance to create something meaningful.

Also, you could get the crabs.

And wouldn't you become a skank too?

Anyway, skanks don't go with nerds.

The Crabs

There had been a rumor going around my freshman year that this one skank girl had the crabs. Which is terrible, whether it's true or not. But what got everyone worried was we were doing the swimming segment in gym, and no one was sure if you could get the crabs from the pool or not. To make matters worse, the regular gym teacher was out, and so we had a substitute with a real bad attitude. Subs seem to be either all in-your-face to keep troublemakers down, or totally passive, figuring if they don't get riled up about anything, no one will bother to cause trouble. Gym subs are almost always in-your-face. So everyone was a little afraid of the gym class sub, but we were a lot afraid of the crabs. So once the sub was done with her "Okay, we're starting swimming today" speech, she ended with "Any questions?" and there was an awkward silence, because everyone had a question, but no one wanted to ask it. Finally someone blurted out, "Are there crabs in the pool?" The sub got a really annoyed look on her face and snottily said, "Uh, no. Any real questions?" Someone else finally chimed up, "No, we mean, are there, uh, crotch crabs in the pool? Someone in school has them and she was in the last class to swim. Can we get them from the

pool?" The sub got very quiet, then started to turn red. "Uh . . . I
mean. . . . No, that can't happen. . . . Okay, let's get on with it."

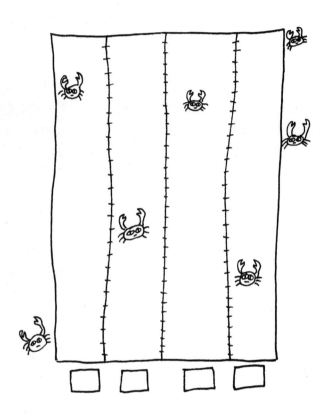

More Crabs

While we're discussing the crabs, there was this one time when my aunt and three-year-old cousin were visiting. My mother and aunt were discussing the perils of public bathrooms. My mother was praising the technique of hovering over the toilet, never allowing your skin to touch the seat. My aunt countered with, "Well, that won't save you from crabs. Crabs can jump."

"So can lobsters," said my cousin, to much merriment.

I don't want crabs, and I totally don't want lobsters. And I'm not even entirely sure what they are, but they seem to be everywhere.

Pay Attention to Omens

I should have known from the very beginning that I was doomed to fail at this asking-out-girls business. Remember that friend of mine who sabotaged my attempts to get to know the girl he also liked? Well, I finally took matters into my own hands and called her myself. I figured she had to have some idea of who I was. Our school wasn't that big, so everyone sort of knew who everyone else was, or could figure it out if need be. I didn't have my license, and I hadn't even considered how we would get anywhere. Have my parents drive us? How mortifying. I really hadn't thought this out.

It went a little something like this one Saturday after-noon (on the telephone, no less):

"Hi, Jen, this is Tom Mayo."

(Pause.) "Hello."

"I was wondering if you wanted to go to the movies to-night."

"I'm busy tonight."

I had not prepared for that.

The next week (on a Wednesday):

"Hi, Jen, this is Tom Mayo."

"Yes?"

"I was wondering if you wanted to go to the movies this Saturday."

"I'm going to the movies with Shelley this weekend."

I was so shocked by the negative answer that I failed to realize there are two more nights per weekend.

The next week (on a Monday):

"Hi, Jen, this is Tom Mayo."

"Hmm-mmm."

"I was wondering if you wanted to go to the movies this weekend."

(Long pause.) "Sure."

Success! Now what? I began to fumble.

"Well, uh, what do you want to see?"

"Just call me Saturday and we'll figure it out."

So I called her Saturday. Every hour on the hour, in fact, because no one was home. I even rode my bike past her house a few times, but no one seemed to be home either. The next Monday she was out of school too. One of her friends came up to me in homeroom and said, "Jen wanted me to tell you that she's not ready to have a boyfriend yet." This I couldn't believe.

"Yeah, fine," I said, only thinly trying to hide my disgust.

So I should have paid attention to the signs: the first girl I ever asked out stood me up. What sort of dating future could I expect starting out like that?

Psycho Route

I'm not sure why, but people really do like riding past the houses of people they like. I don't know what that really accomplishes, or who it impresses.

I suppose that's why Adam refers to this as a "psycho route."

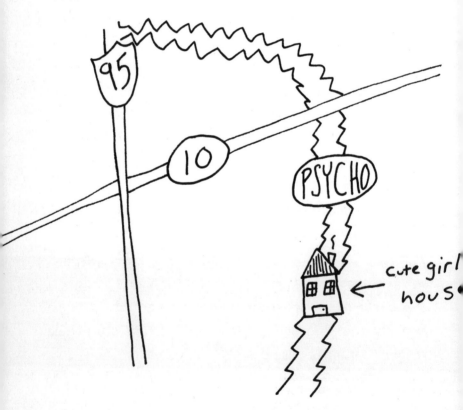

Lab Partners

Amy Montgolfier was one of the girls who confused me more than the others. We sat next to each other in Biology freshman year. In that class the desks were tables that fit two people, and the person who shared your table with you was your lab partner. We were both "M's" so that's how we wound up together. Real scientific. At first, I could really sense that she was not pleased to be paired up with me. But after a while, she seemed to warm up to me, since I made her laugh by making fun of the teacher a lot. He talked with his hands like crazy; it was hard to not do a good impression. So this sort of thing makes me think that if people just got to know me, they'd like me. Could it move from there to "*like* like?" I don't know.

Now if I only could get all the cute girls in school to be my lab partner. It's a start. *Scientific info*

I Hate Other People's Friends

I really do think that Amy Montgolfier liked me. So of course I was very keyed up about the upcoming Thanksgiving dance, in the hopes that this would be the time for me to make my move.

But as you know, I'm prone to problems. This problem came in the form of Tara Pappas, a very short girl who had liked me for some time, despite my repeated dismissals of her affection. Tara was no Amy. I aim high.

The Pappas Affair came to a full blistery head the night of the dance I was so keyed up about. I was biding my time until the first slow dance, knowing that was my chance to move in on Amy. But the time finally rolled around and—gasp!—Amy was hanging around with Tara Pappas! How could I have asked Amy to dance with Tara right there? She might try to intercept me, and I couldn't allow that. Thinking on my feet, I dispatched Steve to send Amy over.

"What?" she shouted over the music.

"Do you want to dance?"

"You know Tara likes you, right?"

"Yeah, so?"

"So she's my friend, and I'm not going to dance with you because it'll hurt her feelings."

"Since when are you friends with her?"

"It doesn't matter, she's my friend, and that's that."

"It's just dancing."

"I said no." And she walked back over to Tara. They whispered to each other and then Tara ran out of the gym, Amy after her. Steve looked at me.

"What's that all about?"

"Amy's being loyal," I said, and walked out of the gym, not looking for Amy or Tara, but out into the night air, wishing it were time to leave.

Things Go Astray

Sometimes the Donkeys turn on each other.

These are good days for the enwedgied masses.

Occasionally they give each other wedgies, or try to. Since they're all pretty much the same size, it's not as easy a game as when they pick on us. Though it is entertaining to see them chasing each other around with their hands down each other's pants. Usually they'll just start punching the hell out of each other's arms in a display of toughness, which seems wed to low IQs. There must be an easier way, like some sort of meter, like one of those hit-the-mallet-to-ring-the-bell things at the carnival, or better yet, like a soil tester, where you just jab the probe ends into their skin and get a toughness reading that way.

One day in particular, they were playing smack-n-poke or grabass or whatever you want to call it, when two of them decided they wanted to show off what excellent fighters they were, and got into a mock boxing match. Everyone gathered around them to form a human boxing ring.

"Biff. Bam. Biffbambam," they said as they threw punches at one another that never connected. They dodged, they danced. It was really annoying. But it finally got a little heated, as Ken Windell got Tommy Flannery "up against the ropes" as it were, basically up against one of the big glass windows that make up Mr. Boort's office.

"He's setting him up for the knockout," Ken said, and threw a not-that-hard punch, but Tommy dodged, and next thing we knew, glass was spraying all over everything and Ken was looking at his hand, which had about a hundred little pieces of glass sticking out of it, and all he could say was, "Ahhhhhh."

Mr. Boort came flying up to the doorway when he heard the noise. "Which peanutheads did this?" Ken couldn't hide. Tommy stepped forward.

"Don't touch your hand—we're going to the nurse," he said, and led Ken out of the room. Tommy followed quietly behind.

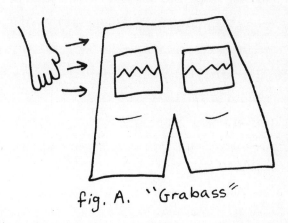

fig. A. "Grabass"

Epilepsy

My mother came into the room. "I just got a phone call from your principal," she said. "Do you know a boy named Larry?"

"Sort of," I said. "He eats lunch with us sometimes."

"Well, I have some news." She paused. "Did you know he was epileptic?"

"No," I said. "I knew he was in Special Ed., but I didn't know why."

"Well, in addition to his learning problems, he was also epileptic. Last night he was drawing a bath and he had a seizure while he was waiting for the tub to fill. He hit his head on the faucet and drowned in the tub. His mother found him when the water started running down the stairs."

Rob Gets the News

I was not looking forward to homeroom the next day. As I had suspected, Rob and Barry were not taking the news well.

"Did you hear about Larry?" Rob asked. "What an idiot!"

"Who drowns in the tub?" said Barry. Then he shook back and forth like he was having a seizure and went "uhuhuhuhuhuhhuh."

"It's not funny," I said. "He died."

"Sorry your best friend died," said Rob. "Hey, Tom, hot enough for you?"

The thing that sucks about homeroom is that you can't just get up and walk out of it. Well, you can, and I tried, but you tend to get in trouble. Which I did.

DETENTION SLIP
Who got busted?
TOM Mayo
That's who got busted

College

I have this hope that college will be different. I mean, you choose to go there, right? High school, you have no choice. That could explain the bad attitudes of a lot of the people there. But college, if people are there by choice, they must be different. They must want to learn. So they're smart. So they should be above all this crap.

It's got to be better. This one time last year I was in Contemporary Government, which was the biggest joke, but you have to take it as a freshman. (Also, I believe it's what they used to call "Social Studies," but "Contemporary Government" sounds more, well, contemporary or something.) No one in that class even tried. One day we had to do this reading about "Old Deluder" laws, and nobody did the reading but me apparently. Basically, it was five pages about how there used to be laws to teach people to read so they could read the Bible, thus escaping the grasp of the Old Deluder. The teacher, Mr. Zerot (pronounced "zero"—very on-target) must have called on every kid in the class trying to get an answer to the question "Who is the Old Deluder?" Most of them just sat there, not even making eye contact with him when he called on them, or maybe just grunting. The really ambitious ones might have gotten an "I don't know" out. But he just kept going.

"Bob, who is the Old Deluder?"

"Sue, who is the Old Deluder?"

"Jimmy, who is the Old Deluder?"

"Ed, who is the Old Deluder?""

"Tammy, who is the Old Deluder?"

"Eustache, who is the Old Deluder?"

Finally, after about twenty people, he got to me.

"Tom, who is the Old Deluder?"

"The freakin' Devil! Jesus! What the hell?"

Which got me a trip to the principal's office. This is what I get for doing the assigned reading.

College HAS to be better than this, right?

Notes

Freshman year I got asked to take notes for one of the other kids in Mr. Zerot's class. I guess he wasn't doing so well in the class, and I was.

"Tom, can I talk to you?" Mr. Zerot said as I was trying to leave.

"Uh, sure."

"I know that you're doing well in this class, and I've noticed that you take a lot of notes. George's parents are concerned about his grade last semester, so I thought you might be willing to copy your notes for him, so he has something better to study from."

"You mean like write them all over again?"

"Oh no, you'd be allowed to use the copier in the office. You could just make copies at the end of the week, or even right after class if you felt motivated."

"I guess so," I said.

"It would really be helpful to George to see good note taking. You're doing the best in this class, so you seemed like a prime candidate."

What he didn't know was that my note taking was actually me working on a comic called "Mr. Zerot vs. Number 1" and it was basically me hitting Mr. Zerot over the head with large objects and people from class. I didn't think there was any way my life could have gotten worse, but there I was.

Copier Privileges

75th Generation
Freshman Year
Class Photo

Mr. Boort

The only upside I could find about taking notes
for George was the unsupervised copier privileges. This
was actually kind of big. Sure, I could make copies at the library
for ten cents each, but here I could make as many as I wanted
for free. I learned that if I went as school was letting out, the
secretaries were too busy dealing with dismissal-related issues
to pay attention to what was going on in the copier room.

I went a little nuts. I made copies of pictures I liked to use
in collages; I made copies of comics I drew and bound them
into books; and I even figured out that if you moved a picture
while copying, it would distort in really cool ways.

As far as the actual note copying, I just ended up giving
them to George in class the next day, so my daily visits to
the copier room didn't arouse any suspicion. He didn't really
care about this whole thing. It was his parents' idea.

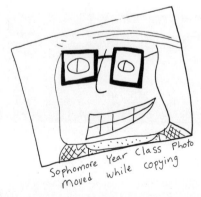

Sophomore Year Class Photo
Moved while copying

Parental Advice on Dating

"Adam's going out with a girl in college?"

"Yes, Mom."

This was a favorite topic of discussion.

"His mother must be out of her mind."

"I think she likes her. Some parents support their children's dating decisions."

"I just think that she'd go crazy with him going out with a girl that much older."

"I don't see why it matters." I pushed my TV tray out of the way and went to the kitchen to get more milk.

"Are you jealous that Adam has a girlfriend and you don't?"

"I don't care."

"Do you talk to girls at your school?"

"Yes, Mom."

"Do you ever think of asking them out?"

"No one there really interests me."

"Well, does Adam's girlfriend have any friends?"

The irony never sank in.

"Yes, Mom, but they're OLDER."

"Well, I just want you to be happy."

"I'm happy with the way things are."

At least once a week we'd have this discussion. Adam's girlfriend was only two years older than him, which was like a senior going out with a sophomore, which wasn't all that uncommon. But because the girl was in college, it seemed to make some sort of big difference. I guess some parents want their kids to be happy no matter what, even if it involves annoying them near to death. I guess that way when they find happiness, at least they'll know what it's not.

only 2 years older!

Tower of bricks made of stuff that makes a big difference

COLLEGE

STAY AWAY, HIGH SCHOOL JERKS!

Videos

The weekend after Larry died, Rob and Barry wanted me to go over to Rob's house. I was still pretty mad at them over the whole Larry thing, but I didn't have any other friends or anything else to do, so I went over anyway.

"You have to see the video we made the other day," Rob said. He opened a file on his computer. The movie came up, and there were Barry and Rob.

"Hi, Larry," Rob said.

"Oh, hi, Rob," Barry/Larry said. "Hot enough for you?"

I opened my mouth to say something, but before I could Barry/Larry started shaking and going "uhuhuhuhuhuhuhuh" and fell over.

Then I was going to say something else, but the screen cut to a new shot, of Rob dressed in orange hunting gear, holding his brother's air rifle. "Yeah, me and Larry used to go hunting, and uhuhuhuhuhuhuhuhuh," and he hit his head on the rifle and fell down.

Rob and Barry were doubled over laughing at themselves.

"You guys are assholes," I said. As I walked out the door,

I could hear more "uhuhuhuhuh" coming out of the TV.

Larry Meant to Be

The more I thought about it, Larry kind of poked a big hole in the whole "meant to be" thing. He spent his whole life being kept away from other kids because he was in Special Ed., and then he died in a bathtub. Why would anyone deserve that? Larry never bothered anyone (except Rob and Barry, and they don't matter). Why can't someone who made other people's lives miserable go die in a bathtub?

Things I Wish I Had Done Before I Died If I Were Larry

Eat lunch without getting picked on.

Go to one last winning Red Sox game with good seats (the good seats part is easy, the winning, maybe not so much).

Kiss a girl.

Not have epilepsy.

Homeroom

Homeroom really sucked for a while after that. Luckily, half-way through the year they allow freshmen to transfer to the Yearbook Homeroom if they want to work on the yearbook. Since that's big with the "in-crowd," that's where Rob and Barry wound up.

Go It Alone

So I couldn't just sit around the house worrying about not having any friends anymore. I mean, I could, but sitting around feeling sorry for yourself starts to get a little old after a while. Also, eventually parents notice and start asking questions. It's best to just get out of the house.

It was a little cold for a bike ride that time of year, but freezing fingers can really take your mind off of other problems.

Who Was Larry?

I guess I didn't even really know Larry, since all I ever did was eat lunch with him a few times, and quietly watch while Rob and Barry were mean to him. I felt guilty about not sticking up for him then; now I feel very guilty. It's not like their making fun of him caused him to commit suicide or something, but if I had known his time was limited, I would have tried to make it a little bit better.

Driving Lessons #1

I'm not sure where my parents found the driving school, but I imagine it has to be the cheapest one. This is obviously reflected in the quality of the instructors. This quality became clear after my first lesson. The teacher spent most of the time staring out the window, and then once in a while he'd mumble, "Uh, turn right, I guess." Eventually we wound up down a dead-end street, so he decided it was time to practice backing up. So I backed up right over a pile of nails that was in the road, which he had failed to notice. "Oh, uh, stop a minute," he said, then he got out and looked at the tires, looked at the pile of nails, looked at the tires, knelt down and felt the tires, looked at the pile of nails, stood up, looked around, scratched his head, then got back in the car. "Better keep an eye on that," he mumbled.

We drove off, and had to pick up the kid who had the next lesson, one town over. The kid was sitting on his front steps waiting, but I laid on the horn, just for the hell of it. "Hey, that's uh, oh, there he is," said the instructor.

"Hey, Carl," said the next kid. "I was worried I was going to have Neil today."

"Yeah, Neil," said Carl.

Then we drove back to my house, listening to the next kid complain about Neil the whole way. Apparently Neil is the Devil, if for no other reason than he actually enforces the rules. Have mercy!

Fun

A good form of entertainment in Shop is if you get to be in charge of cleaning up all the sawdust from under the machines with the giant vacuum. It's a huge accordion-like tube, like the kind that comes out of a dryer, and it runs into a closet and into a giant gray box that has two red buttons, which Mr. Boort has labeled "suck" and "blow" with black magic marker on masking tape. We are only supposed to use "suck," but sucking is boring. The best thing to do is to fill the end of the tube with sawdust and wood shavings and then "blow" them at someone. I could do this all day. Which sort of worries me. What could this possibly mean for my future? Can I major in this in college? Or am I just totally immature?

You really only get away with it once or twice and then Mr. Boort hears the laughing and comes out and yells, "Knock it off, you peanutheads. Clean it up." And then we're still giggling and it means you're picking up a bigger mess than you started with, but it's much more fun than if we had strictly stuck to "suck"ing.

Fun with Currency

Some of the geniuses in class found that the belt sander is powerful enough to bend coins, so they bent all their change. They didn't seem to realize that this was their lunch money they were destroying. I was in line behind one of them when he handed the cashier a handful of coins bent at right angles. The lady just sort of looked at him, and he looked back at the lady like she was the stupid one.

"You can't pay with this," she said.

"It's money."

"It's damaged. The bank won't take this."

He glanced over at me. I gave him a "hey, don't look at me" look. The line began to grow.

"Do you have any other money?"

"No," he said, putting his tray down. He stepped out of line and went off into the lunchroom to mooch money off other people.

"Some people, really," the cashier said to me.

"You don't have to tell me twice, sister," I said.

Then I was the one getting the dirty look.

The Perks of Shop

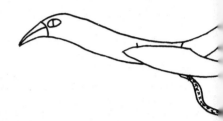

Our parents receive more crappy furniture from our endeavors in Shop class than they could ever want. They can't throw it out without insulting us, but they sure can't have it out where company might see it. Who wants a magazine rack with hearts in the base, especially when that rack is crooked, irregularly stained, and sanded so one edge is round, the other slanted? Our parents are truly torn between parental pride and another type of pride that prohibits the display of C- furniture. Some things are easy to say no to, like the routings of my name and sneaker brand names. Those were obviously to go in my room. The cockeyed desktop bookshelf that's made of three boards that interlocked ("you don't need nails that way") was presented to my father, who insisted that I keep it in my room since I "had more books" than him. Never mind the fact that the thing only held about five books anyway. In our house at least, the magazine rack with hearts in the base (which was actually quite tricky to make—you had to drill two holes for the curved top of the hearts, and then saw the rest, and sand it so it seemed like one fluid cut. That's why they all sucked, it was way too hard) wound up in our basement filled with half-full or dried-up cans of paint and stain in a dank corner by the woodpile. My duck marionette ended up in the back of my closet with some sneakers with holes in them and a deflated basketball. My "wind spiral," which was about thirty thin strips of wood connected by a big screw down the middle, then sawed into a diamond shape, and then you twist each piece of wood out a little bit more than the other so it forms a spiral, was given to my aunt, who gave it to another relative, who gave it to a friend, who gave it to one of her relatives, and then we lost track of it. I never even bothered to make the hanging seagull that you pulled a string in its stomach and the motion made the wings flap. Even I could see that this was useless.

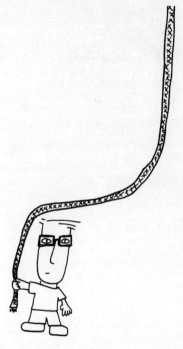

Wampum Belts and the Single Girl

And now we have to make wampum belts.

This is the most useless project so far. No one is going to use this outside of class. But because we all fear failing Wood Shop (really pathetic) we have to do it. The loom is really difficult to make too. There are all sort of dowels that have to move around during the weaving process, and other dowels that are glued in place, and more drilling than we've done all year. There was a brief glimmer of hope when we saw a knife-like object was part of the loom, and many conspiratorial looks were shot around the room. Robert Manly looked as if he were about to wet his pants. But we quickly realized that there wasn't much damage to be done by this item. It was wooden, so none of us were good enough to file it to the point where we could actually hurt someone with it. Mr. Boort was shrewder than he looked. Plus, it's the thing you used to pull the yarn through the weave, so it was always attached to the loom, which made it hard to fight with.

A gloom settled over the class as we began work on this very girly project. The goal should have been to work as quickly as possible to be done with this, but no one could work up that kind of energy. Especially when Mr. Boort tried to make it sound cool by calling them "wampum belts."

One time as I was weaving, Mr. Boort came up to me and whispered, "You know, wampum belts drive women crazy." I looked around the workshop and shuddered at the thought of any of the girls in class being driven crazy by my belt, and I vowed to never wear it around them. Then I imagined myself wearing it to a school dance, wrapped around my waist and knotted jauntily on the side. I burst through the doorway and almost instantly the women attack me, tearing off all my clothes except for the belt as they drag me off to the woods to have their way with me.

Fun with Gym

The only thing worse than wampum belts in Shop was wrestling in Gym class. Swimming was also high up on the list, but since the crab scare did not shut the pool down, someone had broken into the school and tried to fill the pool with Jell-O. The police had a hard time tracking them down, because no one reported having seen someone buying thousands of boxes of Jell-O recently. So whoever did it was smart enough to buy only a few boxes at a time so as not to arouse suspicion. They also must have started collecting the Jell-O in fifth grade in order to have enough, and been incredibly patient. The police never caught them, and while the pool was being repaired, we had an extra unit of wrestling in Gym. Basically, wrestling in Gym is a school-sanctioned assault on the weak. We get into just as many headlocks as usual, but this time no one gets yelled at for it, and there's no opportunity to scream "uncle." You just have to wait until your round is up, or go totally limp and let them pin you. I'd considered falling on my back the minute the whistle blew, but that would only show fear and weakness on my part, as if it weren't obvious enough. The goal was to act like you were fighting, and put up some sort of struggle. That way when you lost, you were still a wuss, but not as much of a wuss as someone who just plain gave up, even though that was what we all wanted to do.

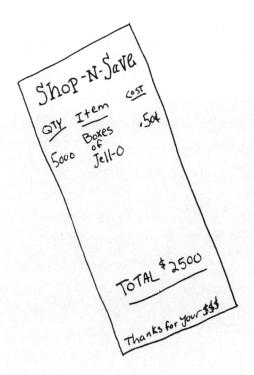

Gym Stuff

One day I forgot my gym stuff, so I had to use a pair of shorts out of the lost-and-found. Even just looking in there makes me feel like I need some sort of shot afterward, but these shorts seemed pretty clean—they were just way too big. Luckily, they had a pull-tie waist, otherwise, I would have been pantsed before I even made it out of the locker room.

"Hey, Miracle Wimp, where'd you get those shorts?"

"Heh," I said. "He was fat, but I was fatter."

"That doesn't even make sense, you asshole."

Lunch

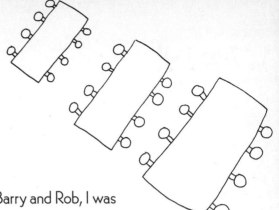

Once I was done with Barry and Rob, I was
kind of done with eating lunch with anyone.
Or I figured I was. I went into the cafeteria the day
after the Larry video expecting to sit by myself. I decided it
wouldn't hurt to give at least a quick look around, then maybe it
might look like I was supposed to meet someone, but they just
weren't there yet. Then I saw Steve and Adam sitting together
at an otherwise empty table. Steve, as I've mentioned, I knew
from kindergarten. Adam and I had gone to camp together a few
years earlier, but we didn't go to the same elementary schools,
so that put an end to any burgeoning friendship. I decided to
take a chance on a couple of people I sort of knew, rather than
sticking it out alone. If it had been warm out, I could have gone
outside and eaten lunch under a tree by myself. But it was the
middle of winter, and you look way more alone without the
tree behind you.

So all I did was ask if I could sit down. They said yes. The
next day I did the same thing. And that was kind of how it
went. As though it were meant to be, you might say. Except
in this case, something good was happening to me.

Friends

So, once Steve and Adam came on board as my friends again, things got a little better. Still, in the back of my mind, I kind of wanted more than two friends. Does this make me greedy? Or was I just paranoid that these guys might someday flake on me too?

Steve, Adam, and Larry

I don't think Adam and Steve would have been mean to Larry. I'm just going on a hunch here. They certainly didn't care about what the "in-crowd" thought. But they did get a kick out of the "in-crowd" story.

"Do you guys want to go to my house after school?" I'd ask.

"Is that what the 'in-crowd' is doing?" would always be the answer.

IN CROWD TO-DO LIST

1. Go to Tom's house
2. Pick on those different from us
3. Continue sucking

Rob and Barry Live On

Even though they weren't in homeroom anymore, I wasn't entirely free of Rob and Barry. This is too small a school to really be able to avoid anyone. And being the type of guys they turned out to be, it wasn't always a good time.

Like the time that I was getting coffee in the cafeteria, but it came out of the coffee machine ice cold. I could feel through the cup that it was ice cold, but just to be sure, I stuck my fingers into it. Just then, Rob, Barry, and a couple of their "in-crowd" friends from the Yearbook Homeroom walked by. "Hey, Tom, hot enough for you?" Rob yelled. And right then I got the feeling that they were going to somehow work this into the yearbook.

The Goon Squad

"The reason we're easily abused," Steve told me at lunch, "is because we're not organized into a cohesive, threatening whole."

"What are you talking about?" I asked him.

"We need a Goon Squad," he said. "If we formed a Goon Squad, we could terrorize this school."

"A bunch of ding-dongs are not going to terrorize anything, no matter how threatening a name they have," I said.

"Maybe so," said Steve, "but regardless, I hereby seize the title of Generalisimo."

"I'll be the Victimizer, then," I said.

Adam came by and sat down. "What are you guys talking about?"

"We're assembling a Goon Squad," I told him. "You can be in it. Pick a title."

"I'd like to be Activities Coordinator," he said. "Just because we're going to strike terror into the hearts of our classmates doesn't mean we shouldn't have a good time. Since I have access to a car, this makes me uniquely qualified."

"You're in," I said.

"So how, exactly, are we going to strike all this terror into all these hearts?" I asked.

"Well," said Steve, "our first order of business should be that no one finds out we're the Goon Squad. If word gets out, we're dead for sure."

"Ah yes," I said. "Nothing says 'terror' like a complete unawareness of terror."

"No reason to single ourselves out any further," he said.

"So, a movie this weekend?" queried the Activities Coordinator.

The Goon Squad Advertises

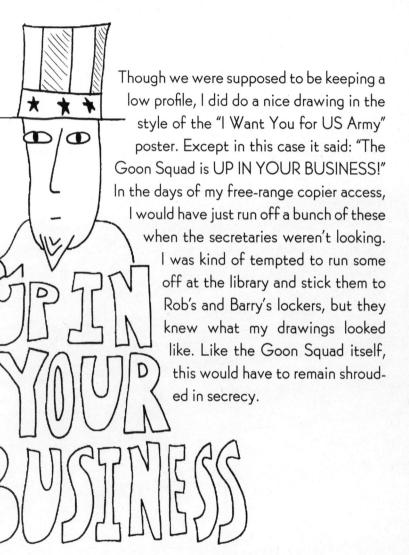

Though we were supposed to be keeping a low profile, I did do a nice drawing in the style of the "I Want You for US Army" poster. Except in this case it said: "The Goon Squad is UP IN YOUR BUSINESS!" In the days of my free-range copier access, I would have just run off a bunch of these when the secretaries weren't looking. I was kind of tempted to run some off at the library and stick them to Rob's and Barry's lockers, but they knew what my drawings looked like. Like the Goon Squad itself, this would have to remain shrouded in secrecy.

Vinnie's Magic Funk

I'm not sure whose it was originally, but at some point, some-one received a bottle of the foulest-smelling cologne ever created. It smelled like kerosene mixed with mouthwash. It also had some name like "Musky Man," but was quickly renamed "Vinnie's Magic Funk" and given a new label thanks to yours truly. As nasty as it was, there were some days after Gym when it actually smelled better than we did, so the bottle was kept in an empty locker in the senior hallway in case any-one needed it.

Br'er Asshole

You've got to watch yourself around the Donkeys.

Marvin Stabone was another one of those people unfortunate enough to get stuck in Shop rather than something safe. Now, I wouldn't say Marvin's retarded, but he's definitely not all there. His brother's seriously retarded—he doesn't even go to school—but Marvin's just a little . . . off. He's a perfectly nice guy, but he's different enough to be a target, and dumb enough that he always falls for whatever the Donkeys are pulling.

So one day, this kid Sean says just loud enough that everyone can hear, "Hey, Tyrone, do you beat off?" (That's another thing—they think it's funny to call Marvin "Tyrone" because it rhymes with Stabone.) Marvin got a little red-faced.

"No," he said.

Sean moved in a little closer. "Come on, Tyrone. Everyone does it, don't you?"

Marvin didn't seem to notice that all the Donkeys were slowly closing in on him. "No," he said again, just staring at the piece of wood he was sanding.

"Hey, it's okay, I beat off this morning before school."

Sean could hardly keep from laughing. "You must do it, everyone does. You beat off, right?"

"Yes," Marvin said quietly.

"Hey, everyone," Sean shouted, "Tyrone beats off!"

Marvin was confused, and the red of shame that was on his face slowly turned to one of rage. "Everyone does," he shouted.

Sean laughed even harder. "No, they don't." He was almost suffocating on his laughter. "No one does."

And that should be reason enough to not trust a Donkey.

The Goonmobile

Even though Adam had access to his parents' car, we started to think we needed an official Goon Squad car, just to seem more menacing.

"A hearse is the only way to go," said Steve. "Associations with death, plus, you can totally blow through red lights at will."

"Where are we gonna get the money for a hearse?" said Adam.

"I don't know," said Steve. "Bake sale?"

"Doesn't having an easily recognizable car defeat the whole idea of remaining anonymous?" I asked. "And we'd either have to all cram into the front seat, or someone would have to lie down in the back."

"Since when are you the practical one?" Adam asked.

"Well, I was also going to suggest that we paint it sky blue, so it blends in with the horizon. By the time you noticed we were approaching, it would be too late."

"That's a good idea," said Steve. "We'll probably have to sell a few extra cakes to be able to afford a paint job, though."

Four Words

There are four words that I never want to have directed at me: "Church parking lot—2:10." Those words would pretty much mean my life was about to meet a violent end. The church parking lot is right next to the far edge of the school parking lot, so it's the closest open space that's not school property, which means if fights happen there, the school can't do anything. I've been to a few fights there, but nothing has ever really happened. It's usually two tough guys staring each other down with a bunch of people watching. Once I saw a guy get his shirt ripped off. He was going to fight a hockey player, and they scuffled for a minute, but the hockey player did that thing that hockey players do in fights. He pulled the other guy's shirt up over his head, but then kept going and pulled it off. At first everyone was excited because it looked like there was going to be an actual fight, but then they became confused at the shirt-pulling, and even more confused when the shirt got pulled off altogether. That was it for the action. Then it was just a shirtless kid staring down a kid with a shirt with a bunch of people watching.

I don't think I would just be staring someone down like

a tough guy were I to grace the church parking lot. I'm not a tough guy, and everyone knows it. No nerd ever challenges another nerd to a fight. No one would go to it, and we have bigger things to worry about than fighting each other, like survival. So if anyone challenged me to a fight, it would most likely be someone who could definitely kick my ass. I'm a wimp. I know it. I'm o.k. with it. I'm just saying that were I to have an appointment at the church parking lot at 2:10, I would be having another one either with the hospital or the morgue at 2:15 or so. Is there wimp insurance? Probably not. No company would take a risk like that.

Teacher Pants

I realize that teachers don't make a lot of money. I'm also aware of the fact that clothes can be kind of expensive. I think they ought to create a special fund so teachers can be provided with new clothes when their ancient polyester pants have shrunk so many times that they leave nothing to the imagination. Nothing. Trig is hard enough, but trying to look at the board when all you can see is your teacher's, er, manliness, makes it much more difficult. Who wants to look up at that? Now, with the creation of my fund, as soon as even the slightest outline is detectable, money would be deposited into a special account at a clothing store, good for one pair of very baggy pants.

Not a trace of "Manliness"

Lucky Star Designer Jeans

Mr. Boort wears designer jeans. They have these stars with wings on the back pockets, and they say "Lucky Star" underneath. The class is united in making fun of these pants. We even made up a little song about them. We'll all be working at our tables, and all it takes is one person to start, and we'll all join in singing, "Lucky STAR designer JEANS!" Mr. Boort acts like he doesn't hear this.

He wears those jeans every day.

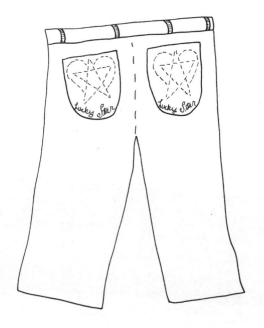

Yearbook Paranoia

I really started to worry about how much of a grudge Rob and Barry could hold. In the school library they had all the yearbooks from every year, and the yearbook people actually got away with some surprising stuff. Like under a picture of a girl with a nose job, they put "the hypotenuse is equal to the sum of the square of the proboscis times ten." But even more surprising was when they listed one senior's activities as "Fudgepacker 1, 2, 3, 4." All it took was one person on the staff to not like you, and I had two. Who knows how I might be remembered?

MAYO, THOMAS
Activities:
Hangin' with Tards
"Hot enough for you?"
Pants wetta 4-eva

The Goon Squad Hit List

The Goon Squad maintained an active list of those who needed "dealing with." Not that we were capable of "dealing with" anyone, but we at least needed to establish who the enemy was. This was NOT written down. We didn't want this falling into enemy hands, or even worse, the hands of a teacher. That was sure expulsion, and trying to explain "imaginative exercise" to any school administrator would surely be a bust. School is the last place for imagination. We wouldn't even have been able to say, "No, it's just like someone's on your 'shit list,'" because then you're in trouble for swearing in school too.

Being a spiteful secret society was not easy. Except for the part where any walk down the hall could result in a new listee.

Mr. Boort's School Photo

What was nice about the library's collection of yearbooks was you could see who had horrible hairdos back in the day (or still had the same horrible hairdo twenty years later), what really old teachers looked like when they were young(er), and the siblings of everyone who had gone through school. It was always interesting to see which ugly people had hot sisters, which hot people had ugly, zitty brothers, and how delinquency seems to run in families.

Anyway, one lazy afternoon I decided I wanted to see what Mr. Boort's pictures looked like. He seemed to have only two photographic moods.

One: Angry Mr. Boort. Brow furrowed, dead-on stare at the camera. You can feel the photographer crapping his pants with fear. Actually, you can almost feel yourself crapping your pants with fear.

Two: Happy Mr. Boort. Eyebrows up, eyes bugged out, big, exaggerated, goofy grin. You can feel the photographer thinking, "What the hell?" However, his pants are clean.

There was only one happy Mr. Boort. That photo day must have coincided with a sale on bouillon cubes.

Mr. Boort

Also Mr. Boort

Candids

Aside from the portraits, the yearbook also has "candids," which are supposed to be these shots of school life, but most of the time they are just as posed as the portraits. Students walking down the hall, but they're all looking at the camera, some giving the thumbs up. Students in the cafeteria line, looking at the camera, holding their noses and "hamming it up." Students in the library, looking at books, making "the thoughtful face." For the most part, the only candids that were always more or less candid were from sports games. There were some that were pretty candid, but they never seemed to come out that well, probably because the photographer was trying not to be noticed, which may not have been the best conditions for good photos. Usually these shots wound up in a collage page, where the badness of the shots was clouded by the sheer amount of photos. As I was looking at one of these, I noticed a small, dark shot of Mr. Boort. It looked like it had been taken through the shop window. I imagine the photographer was probably standing in the bushes, holding the camera over his/her head. I was amazed it actually came out at all. He's running some piece of wood through the band saw, and since it was probably taken after school, he's very focused on what he's doing, rather than making sure the Donkeys aren't dismembering one another. It's a little blurry, but he seems relaxed, and almost content. What does Mr. Boort think about at a time like that? The true meaning of "bolo"? Girls? Band saw safety? Whatever it is, it seems to make the terror of the school day disappear, if even for only a few minutes.

Friendly's

When you don't go to parties because they're full of drunken Donkeys, there isn't much left in the way of entertainment. Fortunately there was some cheap fun to be had. At Friendly's, a bottomless cup of coffee was fifty cents and and a large water was free, as was a plate of pickles. The fools considered them to be some sort of garnish that no one would want a lot of. Steve, Adam, and I could stay there for hours, since we were paying customers, and as long as we didn't act up, they couldn't throw us out. So we often made a night of it. Sometimes we'd talk about how it would be the best date ever to go to Friendly's; you could spend all night with the girl and only have to spend a dollar. Provided your date liked coffee and pickles.

Puds

The model numbers of the carafes that they served the coffee in at Friendly's was either "UD2000" or "PUD2000." None of us could tell the difference between the two models, except that the PUD ones quickly lost their stickers, as we stole them and stuck them on each other.

"Ha! You're a pud!"

Yo-ing

Sometimes after drinking ten cups of coffee you need to get out and do something. Since we didn't like going to parties, the Goon Squad needed another outlet.

I'm not quite sure who originally came up with the idea of "yo-ing," but it caught on real quick. All we did was wait until it was late, drive past someone's house, and beep twice and then yell "Yo!" as loud as you could. It was pretty simple.

That's not to say that there wasn't a huge amount of room for improvisation. The Yo was a classic, but it was always exciting to mix it up. A popular way was to yell the names of your friend's parents, as this was a sure way to piss them off, and to make your friend laugh, because he knew his parents would be pissed. More than a few "Franks!" were shouted at my house because everyone knew my dad hated to be called by his first name. And once, for no real reason, we yelled "Gerbil!" at someone's house.

My favorite was the time I drove past Steve's house and instead of two beeps, I gave the old "shave and a haircut" beep and instead of "two bits" I yelled, "Dicknose!"

This was actually kind of a stupid move, since Steve's

parents were kind of religious. But the next day I saw him in school and it had all worked out.

"My mom said, 'What did he say?' but I wouldn't tell her. She kept bugging me and finally I shouted, 'He said dicknose, Mom!' Then she giggled and said, 'But you're not a dicknose.'"

American Sign Language
for "dicknose"

Run Silent, Run Deep

Adam's parents' car was kind of old. Not wicked old, but old enough that you could actually turn off the headlights. Daytime running lights would be a pox on the Goon Squad.

You needed headlights that could turn off to "run silent, run deep." This is Goon Squad code for "drive with the headlights off." We would do this sometimes if we were trying to "Yo" and needed an extra element of surprise, or if we were driving past a Goon Squad enemy but were unsure of what to do. Sometimes we'd drive past someone's house a bunch of times, bickering about what we should yell, and if we should worry about them recognizing our voices. Eventually, we'd do nothing. They may not have known we were there, but I like to think our presence was felt.

Boating

Once we decided to go boating. There were three of us, and two of us owned two-man inflatable boats. There was a pond in the center of our town, and we figured that was as good as anywhere. We put on our orange personal flotation devices (PFDs), and I managed to dig up a sailor's hat from some old Halloween costume.

We got to the pond and the first boat got out fine. As I was loading in my boat, I turned and saw a very unsmiling cop standing behind me shining a flashlight in my face.

"Tell them to come in," he said.

"Come ashore, mateys!" I hollered.

They came in.

"The park is closed," the cop continued, "and even when it's open, you're not allowed to launch that sort of craft." I couldn't believe that he didn't think this was funny.

We loaded the boats back into the car and set off for someplace else.

Eventually we found a stream a few towns over, but quickly found out that all the trees had branches touching the water, and all these branches had huge clumps of slime on them, which hit every single one of us as we went downstream. We called it quits pretty quickly, and went to Friendly's, still covered in slime and wearing our PFDs, to brag about the evening's events.

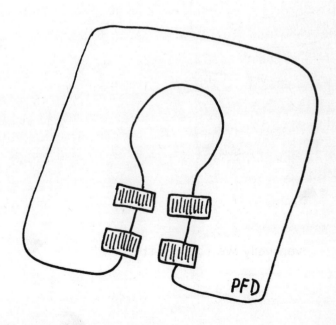

Depression

It's kind of depressing that the most exciting thing I had going on in my life right about then was Mr. Boort and the machinations of the Goon Squad. But I suppose I should be happy there was at least something. Winter can be tough.

PR

Rx: Tom May

INGREDIENT
obsession with
Mr. Boort

Mr. Boort, Small

Mr. Boort, age 1

"What do you think Mr. Boort was like when he was a kid?" I asked Adam.

"How the hell should I know?" Adam said. "He's not even my teacher. He never comes out of the shop, so I've barely even seen the guy."

"I guess," I said. "He's such a weird guy, it's tough to imagine him being anything but Mr. Boort. But something has to have made him this way."

"Yeah, being in combat in the Korean War probably had something to do with it."

"I suppose that's true. But do you think he used to be a Donkey, or one of us?"

"I bet he was a Head," said Steve. "Though, they didn't have heavy metal back then, so I don't know what kinds of t-shirts they would have worn. Perhaps they went shirtless."

"Yeah, maybe," I said. "But my worry is that he was like us, but years and years of torment by Donkeys drove him to bouillon cubes and making up insulting names for people."

"You mean like 'Donkeys'?" said Adam.

"See, it's happening to me already," I said.

Driving Lessons #2

So of course I had to get Neil for my next lesson. I don't know what that other kid's problem was. Neil was a big guy and had a Russian accent, but he actually seemed to pay attention to your driving. He also liked to sing along to classic rock radio. "Takingk care oov biznEZZ!" while slapping his leg in time, but not really. "Now you vill take me to my mechanick," he said after we had practiced not backing up over nails and a few three-point turns. He directed me to this rundown industrial part of town I had never seen before, and into this junkyard, which apparently was also a mechanic. "You vill vait here," he said, and walked into this shack that must have also been a garage. He came out a few minutes later, not looking happy. "My car iz not ready," he said. "Ve go back to your house now." I put the car in gear and started to drive, but this stupid pigeon was in my way, and just kept waddling along ahead of the car and not flying away. I didn't know what to do, so I figured if it was going slow, I could get it between the wheels and drive over it without hurting it. I lined it up down the middle of the car and punched the gas.

"You don't like pigeons?" Neil asked.

"I thought it would get out of the way," I said.

"He vas not a smart bird, no," said Neil.

I looked in the rearview mirror, and there was the pigeon waddling along behind me like he was still the only thing for miles around.

Not a smart bird, no

Drive-by

One night I was sitting in my room listening to music. It was a nice night and I had my window open. It was kind of late, so there wasn't much traffic. So it was kind of noticeable when a car came slowly driving down the street. When I heard the slow roll, I looked out the window. Even with its headlights off, I could tell it was Rob and Barry in Rob's dad's car. It was the only giant gold Mercedes in town, and the color was really reflective under the streetlights. I don't know if they saw me there in the window, but they probably would have yelled "Miracle Wimp" at the house anyway. Knowing I was there watching it only made it better somehow.

Night Before the License Test

I don't usually get too nervous about stuff. Little kids with paintball guns, going to the library when it's full of Donkeys, that's really about it. But I was incredibly nervous about the driver's license test. But I guess that's because I had so much riding on it. Like, if I didn't get my license, I wouldn't get a girlfriend, and I wouldn't be able to escape this awful town. The thing that sucks is that being nervous made me not able to sleep, and not sleeping was making me more nervous, because then I got to worrying that I would fail because I was too tired. Then that worry fed into all the other worries, making it even harder to sleep, and on and on.

It sucked.

I think I may have slept for a little while, but then I just had nervous dreams. When you're that tired, it's hard to tell what's a dream and what's just lying there being paranoid. I seem to remember stuff about girls wanting to go out with me, but then changing their minds when they found out I had failed my license test.

Test

I don't know why I was so worried about my driver's license. When I went to take the test, there were two other people taking it with me. One was just some guy who didn't really say much. He was wearing a t-shirt that said SKATE OR DIE, and I was worried that if this was the case, getting his license might kill him. The other was this really tiny girl. She was as short as she was just skinny, and she had this frizzy hair that stuck out all over the place, so she kind of looked like a broom turned upside down. I can totally drive better than a broom. Well, I guess it's not a competition, but maybe sometimes if someone is so bad at driving they can distract from other people's mistakes because they are so ridiculous. Like when it was broom girl's turn to take the test, she couldn't even open the window to do her hand signals. She had to use both hands, and could really only get the handle turned halfway at a time. She'd have to puuuuuuuuuush . . . half turn, adjust her hands and then puuuuuuuuuull . . . half turn. Adjust her hands, puuuuuuuuuuuuush . . . half turn. It took her like ten minutes to even just open the window. I wished that I had gone after her so when my turn to open the window came I could have rolled it down with one hand and kind of given the registry cop a nod to let him know I was totally in control of my destiny. But I had already gone, so maybe she at least erased anything I had done wrong from his memory.

License

All three of us were sitting in the lobby of the DMV. Me, Broom Girl, and Skater Dude. Nobody really said anything because we were all so nervous. They don't tell you whether you've passed when you're in the car, they make you come in and wait. So we were in there for like five minutes, and the DMV guy was in some office talking to someone. We could hear a lot of laughing, which seemed good, but we couldn't make out what anyone was saying. He could very well have been laughing about what a horrible bunch of drivers he just took out for their tests. Me and Skater Dude kept making frightened eye contact. Broom Girl was off in her own little world.

There was another burst of laughter, then we heard someone say, "Alright, I guess I'll tell them." Skater Dude sat up really quickly and got this wide-eyed freaked-out look on his face. I realized that it was probably also the same look I had on my face.

Broom Girl stared off into the distance, unaware that anything of importance was about to take place.

The DMV guy stepped out of the room. He was smiling, but quickly switched to a very stern look.

Oh crap.

But he couldn't hold it for very long. "Congratulations, kids," he said, smiling, and he handed us our certificates that said we passed.

Why do people do that sort of thing? I bet he does that to everyone and never gets tired of it.

License Photo

I decided I wanted to look really tough in my license photo. I figured that way if I got pulled over, the cop would look at the picture and think twice about hassling me. I had forgotten about the whole there-is-no-way-I-can-look-tough thing I have going for me. I sort of look like I'm squinting, or really sleepy. Totally non-threatening.

I originally was going to try to make some stupid face just to be funny, but then I realized if I got pulled over I'd have to make that exact face in order to avoid trouble.

"No, officer, it really is me."

Contorts face.

Downside

The downside of having my driver's license is that it means I can get a job. Or, actually, I have to get a job. I don't really want one, but gas isn't free, you know, and we're not here to provide you with the Tom Mayo No Charge Transportation Network. Of course, if I have a job, I'll need the car to get there, and it will be tied up the whole time I'm at work, or they'll have to drive me there and pick me up if they want the car, which seems an awful lot like a transportation service to me. But my father is going to ask around and see if he can find me anything, and I don't really have much of a say in this.

Computers

This idea has really been bugging me.

"Do you guys think there's some sort of giant computer that determines everyone's lot in life?" I asked one day at lunch.

"What are you going on about?" asked Adam.

"Well, I got screwed out of Animation because of a computer error. Am I getting screwed out of life because of the same sort of thing?" I clarified.

"If such a thing exists, do you think it's like a big mainframe, or just like a spreadsheet on a desktop somewhere?" asked Steve.

"A mainframe?" said Adam. "The Galactic WANG?"

"Oooh, bonus for the old-school WANG reference!"

The two of them were really enjoying themselves.

"Yeah, a desktop would probably crash too much and be prone to viruses," said Steve when he stopped laughing.

"I'm kind of serious," I said. "If this sort of thing exists, how do I get my status changed?"

"I'd think you'd need to talk to the Admin," said Steve. "He's the only one with the privileges to make those changes."

Leave Town

"I met some cool people this weekend," Adam said.

"Oh really," I said. "Did they import some?"

"No, they're not from here, obviously," he said. "They live in Westfield. I met them at the record store in Northampton."

"Hmm," I said. "I guess that place attracts cool people from miles around."

"Well, you've got to go somewhere to get away from the Donkeys and the music they love. Sadly, Donkeys seem to exist in all towns. Some just isolate them better."

"Indeed," I said.

"Well, anyway, I'm going to hang out with them on Saturday if you want to come. If nothing else, it's a change of scenery. And no one there knows us."

"Yes, their taunting will be less informed," I said.

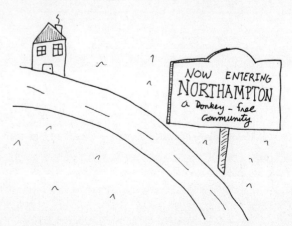

Payback Time

"I got my license."

"Well, hey," said Adam. "Maybe now you can cart ME all over town."

"Uh, okay," I said.

"Now when is Steve going to get his? I'm tired of driving him to get cigarettes. Buying me a soda is small compensation for having to smell his smoky ass there and back."

"Sheesh, you're real cranky today."

"I think I need caffeine. Come get me, let's go to Friendly's, get all coffee'd up and drive around. I want to take in the sights I miss because I'm always driving."

Chess

"I'm getting my ass kicked in Chess all year," said Adam. He came to a stop sign, looked both ways, then kept driving. (Turns out he prefers to be in control.) "Good thing my grade is based largely on showing up. That I can totally do. How's Shop treating you?"

"Ugh," I said. "It's like Gym with tools. I mean, aside from the tools that already take Gym."

"Nice."

"Actually, if not for the constant struggle to survive, I might actually enjoy it."

"Really?" Adam seemed surprised.

"Well, Mr. Boort seems to think I'm okay, so at this point I can pretty much do stuff on my own."

"What have you done?"

"Well, I made a big plaque that says ASS. I didn't say I was making good use of my time. But at least now I have a Christmas present for my father."

"What did Mr. Boort have to say about the plaque?"

"He didn't even notice. He's too busy chewing bouillon cubes or keeping the Donkeys from running rampant. I could

be making a bomb and he wouldn't notice, because he's decided I'm not dangerous. This lack of attention is strangely
liberating."

Pants! Pants! Pants!

Adam's birthday was coming up, so I was looking for a stupid gift for him. As usual, this brought me to the 99-cent store. Not everything in the store was actually 99 cents. At one point it was, but then for some reason they changed their minds. When the store advertises "Yes, Everything Is 99 Cents!" and people constantly ask, "How much is this?" you're bound to give up at some point.

So I was looking at all the hideous little figurines of clowns and stuff, and dolphins with clocks in them, and then I just happened to glance over at the clothing rack.

And there they were.

Lucky Star Designer Jeans.

I have been burnt by pants before, but there was no way I could not buy these. Even though they weren't 99 cents.

Lord of the Pants

"Dude," Matt Trumbull said as he was standing behind me. I was fully expecting a wedgie, so I whipped around as quickly as I could. I didn't know why he said "dude" if he was sneaking up on me, but some people just aren't smart.

"Where did you get those pants?" he said.

Then I realized that I was wearing my Lucky Star Designer Jeans. This is like when I wear a t-shirt with a stupid saying on it, and then wonder why people are giving me weird looks.

"Uh, Mr. Boort made me promise not to tell so his supply doesn't dry up."

"Dude, that's awesome."

So, when I try to be cool, I get hassled. When I try to be an idiot, people think it's cool. This makes no sense.

Adam re: Jeans

"So they make fun of Mr. Boort for the jeans, but they think it's cool when you wear them?"

"Yes," I said.

"Do they know you're joking?"

"I don't think so. I don't think they're that smart."

"Hmm. Well, it's cool that you're possibly safer because of this, but by all means DO NOT start hanging out with these guys."

"Yeah, they don't think it's THAT cool."

Gilbert

The guy Gil that Adam met was pretty okay, once I finally got to meet him. I wouldn't say he's a nerd necessarily (not that I consider any of us nerds either, but I'm just passing along the consensus), but he'd definitely be considered a weirdo at our school, and the Donkeys don't break it down into subgroups. He's into art and stuff, and we all know that's not cool.

"So, do you guys get hassled by Donkeys, er, I mean 'cool kids'?" I asked him.

"Heh, Donkeys," he said. "I guess we do. There's enough of us that we try to stick together. Maybe they'll yell some crap at the group, but they'll leave us alone as individuals."

"We're too fragmented, then," I told Adam. "Perhaps the Goon Squad needs to enlist more members."

"Yeah, that's all you," said Adam. "What's worse, getting picked on, or hanging out with the less fortunate?"

"Well," I said. "I guess we'll have to be picky. Nerds and dorks will be okay, but we'll have to draw the line at feebs."

"You spearhead this campaign and get back to me," said Adam.

Downside, Part II

So my dad found me a job as a janitor at the health club he goes to. It's only one day a week, but the shift starts at six in the morning on Sunday. I suppose the good thing is that no one will see me there, since I doubt anyone in high school is up at six on a Sunday.

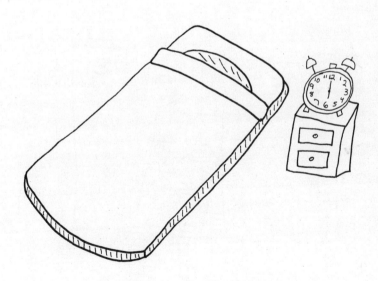

Training

So I got there at six on my first day. No one was there to meet me. I waited and waited, and I had no idea what to do because I'd never met anyone from this health club, so I wouldn't even have known who to call or complain to. Finally, at around twenty after, a car pulled up and let some guy out, and he walked over to the front doors where I was sitting in the cold all that time. Glad I got there early.

Training, Part II

Patrick, my new boss, was late because he had been out drinking. Also, at some point in the night he had gotten into a fight and seemed to think that his face was all messed up. I know this because he wouldn't stop looking at himself in the mirror. "So what you do is spray the cleaner on the counter . . ." (looks at both sides of his face in the mirror) ". . . and then you, uh . . ." (leans in for a better look) ". . . wipe it down . . ." (turns head from left to right) ". . . with, uh . . ." (right to left) ". . . a paper towel." It went on like this for the whole four hours. The whole gist of it is, take out the trash, wipe the counters, mop the showers, and vacuum anything that has a carpet on it. I could have been trained in ten minutes. But it took four hours, and I still had to come in on Saturday the next week to train with the regular morning guy.

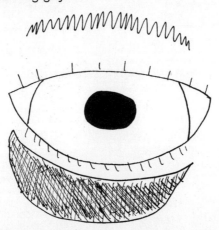

The Morning Guy

The morning guy was a competitive bodybuilder. He was also barely five feet tall, which meant he was almost as wide as he was tall. Should I mention that he was almost completely bald, but what hair he did have was long? Might as well. It also looked like he used to have a rat-tail but grew it all out. Hot. Anyway, he at least showed up on time, but mumbled so much I could barely hear what he was saying (could be the long distance sound had to travel from his mouth to my ear). But basically I just did what Patrick showed me to do while Morning Guy flexed in front of the mirror.

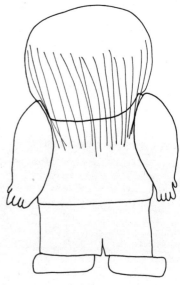

Fighting

The "one break a day" Cigarette
Takes 3 hours to smoke!

Training went on for a couple of weeks for some reason. Patrick likes to talk a lot. Patrick is also full of it. This makes it really hard for me to pass up some of the comedic opportunities. The fact that Patrick will get fired if he hits me makes it that much harder to resist.

"If you're going to be a smartass, I'm gonna have to teach you how to fight dirty. You're too much of a scrawny little shit to win a fight otherwise," Patrick told me.

"Didn't you just get your ass kicked like two weeks ago? I'll take lessons somewhere else, thanks."

"That's what I'm talking about, asshole. I should kick your ass for that."

"Then you'd lose your job on top of having gotten your ass kicked."

"You're a fucker. I'm going outside to have a cigarette."

And that's how I ended up cleaning the whole club on my own again. Long cigarette.

Shirley Temples

After a while Patrick decided that I was able to deal with opening the club on my own. I guess it gave him more time to sleep off whatever beating he had gotten the night before. But as I may have mentioned, this job was not difficult—two people weren't necessary. Plus, with Patrick out of my hair, I could kick back a little. I'd make announcements over the intercom like, "Hey, annoying guy in the locker room, how about putting your dirty paper towels in the trash," and I was free to sample the wares behind the bar. While I might have been a whiz at janitorial duties, my bartending skills were lacking. Or maybe booze is just nasty. I don't know. What I do know is that Shirley Temples are quite easy to make and very delicious. I don't know if anyone at the club noticed that we seemed to be going through a lot of grenadine. And I'm pretty sure no one saw me, vacuum in one hand, Shirley Temple in the other, going about my morning duties.

Yearbook Cuties

Sometimes before I got my license, when Adam was off with Becky, I'd just sit in my room and listen to music and look through the yearbook at girls' pictures and think if any of them might like me. Sometimes, if I thought there might be even the slightest possibility, I'd feel all lightheaded. Then if I saw the girl in school, I'd get all freaked out, like she might somehow know I do this.

Later, I'd sometimes hear the songs I'd listen to while doing this in the car, and that lightheaded feeling would come back all by itself.

First Paycheck

Well, after all that training and picking up after jerks, I finally got a paycheck. You know what? Working twelve hours a week for minimum wage does not get you a lot of money. And then they take taxes out of that. Good thing I was no longer saving for expensive army pants (they're "out" now anyway).

In celebration of this huge windfall, I bought a tank of gas and one of those deodorizer trees for the rearview mirror, which I threw out five minutes later because it gave me a terrible headache.

So here's what I've got going for me: license, car (sort of), job. Still no girlfriend. Marginally more money.

HEALTH CLUB BANK
PAY To THE ORDER of TOM Mayo
Sixty and 00/100 ___ $60.00
MEMO: Sucker!   health club

Lunch

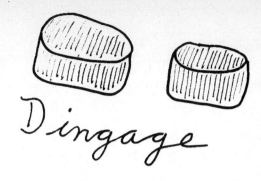

Dingage

We were sitting in the "senior cafeteria," which really only holds about twenty people, but it's off in its own little glassed-in area. I took to calling it the Solarium after my father was in the hospital with an infection. There was a solarium on his floor, and I liked the way it sounded. Anyway, not many seniors even hang out in there. Seniors were allowed to leave school grounds as part of the "Senior Responsibility Program," so of course they did, even if only to eat a bag lunch in the parking lot. So anyway, there we were. We being me and Adam. I had been telling Adam about my new job. "So, basically, Patrick's a Donkey, but without school."

"They're everywhere. I wish they would die when they graduate. If you think about it, their life ends once school does anyway," Adam said.

At that point, Steve walked over with his hand out.

"What the hell do you want?" Adam asked.

"Bestow some dough?" said Steve.

"What the hell?" Adam said.

"Give me some change," Steve clarified.

"What do you need it for?" Adam asked, grudgingly fish-ing around in his pocket.

"I'm gonna dog some Dingage," Steve said.

Adam and I looked at each other.

"I want to get some Ring Dings," Steve clarified again.

Adam gave him a handful of change. Steve turned his hand to me. I dropped a few dimes into his palm, and he happily wandered off to the vending machines.

"Even though Donkeys never really go away, I think it gets easier to avoid them once you're out of school. One of my neighbors is like fifty, but you can totally see he used to be a Donkey. He's just fatter and older. But I don't have to see him in the locker room in his underwear, and he's not going to whip me with a towel. Though, once in a while he passes out on his front lawn. That's what tipped me off."

"I suppose without the inconvenience of football practice, one can focus solely on drinking."

Steve came back, having already crammed one whole Ring Ding into his mouth. "What are you guys talking about?" he asked, spitting chocolate at us.

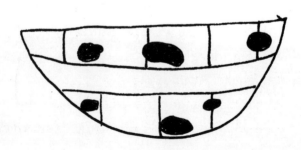

Steve's Take

"We're talking about what Donkeys become when they grow up."

"Cops. Coaches. Fat ex-Donkeys," said Steve.

"So we're agreed on that part," I said. "Do you think they can change?"

"I doubt it. Maybe one or two of them see the light, but why would they want to change? They've got everything they could want right now. By the time they realize there's more to life than being a popular tough guy in high school, it's too late. At that point we've won."

"Viva los losers," I said.

COPS   COACHES   FAT EX-DONKEYS

ALL HATE YOU

175

Driving

You know what else sucks about driving? Now I have to do stuff. Tom, drive to the store and get milk. Tom, go pick up my prescription. Tom, take me to the mall. Then there's the whole having-to-share-the-car thing. So I can drive, but I can't always actually drive.

Flyer

"What's this?" I asked. There was a flyer taped to my locker.

"Oh, the Spring Dance," said Adam. "Your favorite band Synovia is playing."

"What the hell?" I said.

"Well, they are all on Student Council, so I'd assume that has something to do with it."

"Man, those guys have such attitudes as it is," I said. "They don't need this sort of attention."

"I imagine that this won't go over very well," said Adam. "Sure, it's attention now, but it'll bite them in the ass once everyone sees how terrible they are."

"I don't know," I said. "People like some horrible crap. This could be bad."

"Oh, it'll be bad," said Adam. "Delightfully bad."

Mr. Boort vs. the "In-Crowd"

I wonder if Mr. Boort ever had to deal with the "in-crowd." I mean, he has to deal with them daily. Since some of them are in Shop. But when he was the mysterious "little" Mr. Boort, what did he do? Has he spent his whole life being mocked for his Lucky Star Designer Jeans? (Has he been wearing them his whole life? I don't think that even the owner of the Lucky Star Designer Jeans Company has done that.) I guess he's pretty o.k. with himself. He takes a lot of crap over those pants, but he still wears them. He takes a lot of crap from people about everything, but he still goes on being Mr. Boort. Maybe he can't afford better pants, but he doesn't have to go around calling people peanutheads or eating bouillon cubes. Or maybe he does. There could be heroin in the cubes or something. I'll have to ask the Heads about this.

Post-Gym Bouillon Report

I am assured that no one—no one—puts heroin in bouillon cubes.

Synovial Dance

We really weren't sure what to expect with Synovia playing at the dance. We suspected it would be awful, and if it wasn't, the Goon Squad might need to make it awful.

Luckily, they made it pretty awful themselves. In the interest of showing what good musicians they were, they felt the need to "jam out" the introductions to every song, which led to a guessing game. Sometimes we had to wait until they were done and told us what it was before we knew, and we didn't always believe them.

"They said it was Stevie Wonder," I said. "I almost sort of think it may have been."

"I'm pretty sure they just made that one up," said Steve. "They only said it was Stevie Wonder to make it harder to hate."

"Jazz it up!" shouted Adam.

Stevie Wonders
What Song of his
they Just ruined

Other Towns

So we went one Saturday to hang out with Gil and his friends, and they wanted to make a talk show. Someone had a video camera. "You can be the sidekick," Gil told me. I guess there's no better way to make a first impression than to act like an ass and have it immortalized on videotape. And lucky for me, even before the show began I had to do a commercial. Gil decided I had to do one for the local newspaper.

"Come on, just say something funny," he said, handing me a newspaper and shoving the camera in my face.

"Uh, what a gas the *Union-News* is," I began to mumble. "It's got news, it's got crosswords, it's got comics." But I couldn't remember anything else it had until the jingle popped into my head. So I shut my eyes, and as soulfully as I could belted out, "Stay up to date with the weather, the *Union-News*, there's none better."

"Perfect," said Gil, laughing as he shut off the camera.

Wacky Sidekick

So I took my place next to the host's desk. This meant that I had to be on camera all the time, while everyone else only had to make little cameo appearances. I had never met the host before, so that would make our attempts at witty banter that much more awkward. Very early on in the show, it fell on me to do a trick.

"So, Tom"—Abby, the host, turned to me—"do you have any tricks you can do?"

Panic set in. I eyed an Abe Lincoln perfume bottle bust that was a decoration on her desk.

"Well, I don't, but I know my good friend Abe here has one that's quite impressive."

I picked up Abe, and in a high squeaky voice said, "Did someone say 'slavery'?" Then I twisted his head around while making an "ahhhhhh" sound. Everybody seemed to think it was much funnier than it was. Abby even turned to it when she couldn't think of anything to say later in the show.

Cute Audience Members

So there was a very cute girl in the crowd of potential guests/studio audience members. But I never expected her to talk to me after the show.

"That was good, what you did with the Abe Lincoln head."

"Uh, thanks. I was under a little pressure."

"Abby's parents have had that thing forever. I didn't think I'd ever appreciate it."

"Well, I'm happy to have injected new life into it for you."

"I'm Heather."

"I'm Tom."

"Hi."

"I think you already know Abe." And I spun his head around again. She giggled. Maybe it was kind of funny.

Watching the Video

Finally at the end of the night, we got to see the final product. It seemed like we had been there forever and now we had to sit through the highlights of forever. People still laughed at the Abe thing even though by now they must have seen it a million times. I did get to see that Gil had to coax Adam into doing an ad by saying, "Come on, Tom had to sing." Everyone laughed at that more than they laughed at Abe. But I guess in a way they were still laughing at me.

To be honest, I wasn't really paying attention to the video. I knew what was there already, and I couldn't stop thinking about Heather. Sure, we'd only said a few things to each other, but isn't that really all it takes? That seemed to be all it was taking with me.

Oral Sex with Gilbert

Adam and I were visiting again about a week later. We'd been out doing not much of anything, just sitting around drinking coffee and eating pickles, and we decided to drive out to see Gil. It was a half hour away, but we were all about wasting time that night. Spring was here, so it was a nice night to be driving, and we were full of coffee.

We drove by Abby's house first since that was sort of their headquarters because it was the biggest house any of them lived in. Sure enough, Gil's car was there.

Just as we walked in, plans were changing.

"We're going to my house to go swimming," Gil said, so Adam and I got back into his car, and then Abby, Gil, and Heather (!) piled into Gil's car and we followed him to his house.

When we walked into the house Heather said, "Well, we may as well just stay over here since it's late. I'd better call my mother." She grabbed the phone and dialed.

"Mom, Abby and I are going to stay over at Gil's. What? No, Mom. *No*, Mom. Yes, Mom, oral sex with Gilbert, that's right," she said with a smile and a tone that said they'd had this conversation a million times before. I hated the fact that Adam and I had such early curfews.

Unless she was serious about the whole oral sex with Gilbert thing. I so hope she is not a skank.

Gilbert

Swimming

"Are you guys going swimming?" Gil asked.

"We don't have suits," Adam said.

"We always just swim in our underwear," Gil said. "It's dark out, so no one cares."

"I don't know how much longer we can really stay," Adam said, looking at his watch. "It's getting late and it takes a while to get home."

Heather and Abby stood in the background, waiting.

"Do you want to just jump in?"

"I don't know if we should get my parents' car all wet," Adam said.

I started to grind my teeth. Why'd we come out here to do nothing, and why was getting home on time more important than swimming in our underwear with girls?

"Hey, if we towel off, we won't get the car that wet, and we won't be that late," I said.

Adam fidgeted. "My parents are really anal about their car."

I snorted.

"What?" he said.

I didn't want to make a scene in front of everyone, but I really didn't want to leave. Not yet. But I didn't want Heather to think I was some sort of hothead. But I really didn't want to leave her there with Gil, but I guess if oral sex was going to happen, it was going to happen. I just had to hope it wouldn't.

Boners

"You realize if you had gone swimming in your underwear with those girls, you totally would have gotten a boner," Adam said as we were driving home.

"You're probably right."

"You should really thank my parents for being so uptight when we get back."

Stickers

And then there was the day I came down and found a sticker on my locker of a jar of Miracle Whip that had been altered to say—guess what?—"Miracle Wimp." Yep. Someone had some time on their hands. Where might there be a place that you can alter pictures and make stickers? Maybe the Yearbook Homeroom? Sure, lots of people have this stuff at home, but come on. At least they were smart enough to not throw in a "Hot enough for you?"

I got it off, but there's still some sticky crap all over the front of my locker, just to remind me.

Steve's Car

"So the good news," Steve said, "is that I got a car."

"Where'd that come from?" I asked.

"My grandfather is too blind to drive now," he said. "Meanwhile, I am reasonably sighted."

"I've heard that about you," I said. "What's the bad news, then?"

"Well, like you, I now have to get a job because of this," he said. "Also like you, my father got me a job. I'm a busboy at Rebozo's now."

"Sheesh," I said. "Fancy."

"Yeah, I'm not happy about this," he said. "Friday and Saturday nights are gone now."

I had not been expecting this. "Oh. Looks like mine are pretty gone, then, too."

"Sorry," he said. "There's still another bright side, though."

"Which is?"

"My grandfather smoked a lot, so my car already smells like cigarette smoke. I'm in the clear!"

Crud

The Steve news wouldn't have been so hard to take if I could count on Adam to be around, but I couldn't. Lately Becky Frunecki had either dropped a class or was just blowing off a lot of work, because Adam was spending a lot more time with her, especially on the weekends. So now I had a car, but nowhere to go and no one to go there with.

It's not like Steve was going to work at some crappy pizza place where I could go hang out. It's a fancy restaurant, and anyway, now that I think about it, I don't want to be "that guy."

So I guess I need to come up with a plan.

HEY HOW'S IT GOING GUYS? HOW MANY PIZZAS DO YOU MAKE A NIGHT? WHAT DO YOU DO WITH PIZZAS THAT PEOPLE ORDER BUT DON'T PICK UP? HUH? I ONCE ATE A WHOLE PIZZA HOLY CRAP DID I Get SICK

Heather's Phone Number

I didn't have Heather's phone number. I had to call Adam to get Gil's phone number, and then get it from him. Gil can be a pain in the ass.

"Gil, do you have Heather's phone number?"

"What do you want that for?"

"I want to call her."

"What for?"

"To talk."

"What about?"

"Things."

"What sort of things?"

"I don't know."

"How are you going to talk to her if you don't know what you're going to talk about?"

"Just give me the number."

"Are you going to ask her out?"

"I don't know, I just want to talk to her."

"About what?

"About what her last name is." If I had this, I could call information and get her number, hassle-free.

"That's a stupid topic. You're going to bore her."

"JUST GIVE ME THE FUCKING NUMBER!"

"Hey, take it easy, man, you're going to give yourself an aneurysm. I'm not going to give you her number if you're in this kind of mood."

Heather and the Phone

I think I'm definitely going to have to get over this phone thing.

I think I'm okay with that.

The Problem with Dates

The problem with dates is it seems like you always have to do something special. Eventually if things work out, you'll probably just end up hanging out at Derondo's, but for some reason you're never allowed to start there. At least in my limited experience this is how it works.

A real problem arises when the person you want to ask out lives in another town. In a way this could be good, because they don't know that Derondo's is your Derondo's. But you don't want to go on a first date somewhere where everyone knows you're out with an out-of-towner, especially someplace where a Donkey could just walk in a ruin the evening. It's probably best to seek out other entertainment possibilities.

Since Heather was pretty much like me, I knew she had to like Northampton. It was a little out of the way, but it was the only place around that had any decent book or record stores, and they were always fun to go into. At least I thought so. There were all sorts of other types of stores to go into, and we could always just sit on a bench somewhere and people-watch. When you don't have a lot of money, the things you can do are pretty limited.

It's tough when you don't know the town that the other person is from. Maybe they have a Derondo's that's better than Derondo's. It would be more exotic to me because I'd never been there, and it would be better for her because she'd be there with me. But the whole Donkey thing comes up again. Every town has Donkeys.

Also, she didn't drive. That threw a real damper on doing anything in my town, unless I wanted to go get her, drive her back to my town, and then drive her back home at the end of the night. Northampton was definitely the way to go. She was on the way to it, and I could drop her off on the way back. Perfect.

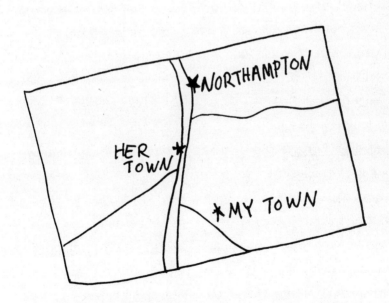

Badminton

Unfortunately for him, Robert Manly didn't just get abused in Wood Shop. The nerd hierarchy extended to anywhere that the opportunity for nerd-on-nerd violence presented itself. Usually Gym class was open season on any and all nerds (all the more so if you wore pink sweatpants), but occasionally we were split up into small-enough groups that we could pick on each other. The same principle as in wrestling applied. There was no way Coach could keep track of everything that was going on at once, so when the time was right, Robert would become a shuttlecock target. Coach was fairly occupied with the Donkeys constantly yelling, "Gimme the cock!" or he just figured there wasn't all that much damage we could do in badminton, so sometimes he'd leave us alone in the gym altogether. At which point we'd whack the birdie at Robert as hard as we could. The good thing about it was that Robert would just usually try to get out of the way rather than whack at the birdie, so not only would we get to abuse him, we'd also win the game. When Coach was looking, we'd point at Robert with our rackets and shout, "I want YOU!" so Coach thought we were really using a psychological offense, and that was why Robert was so rattled. Fortunately, birdies don't leave any sorts of marks, so Coach couldn't be alerted to our strategy by bruises, and we went on to our most successful unit in Gym.

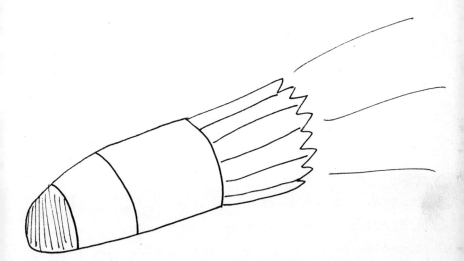

Tennis

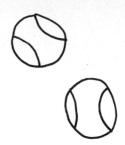

Tennis, of course, was no better. The balls were bigger, and therefore more painful. It was nicer because we were outside. And what made it most fun of all, was hitting the ball as hard as we could and shouting "into the Green Monster!" just like at the Red Sox games as the ball smashed into Robert, who wore the same green t-shirt to gym in the warmer months.

It's a game of love

Get Big

One day I had to go to the health club to pick up my pay-check after school. I didn't have the car that day because I wasn't working, so I had to walk. It's not very far from school, but I have this paranoia about walking down the street. I guess I've had just one too many things yelled at me by carloads of Donkeys. So to lessen the threat of this, I decided to cut behind some stores and through a vacant lot. Of course, as soon as I got though the hedge that obscured all this from view, I came across Chris Carlotta, a Head, and his girlfriend (see SKANKS). Chris was not a Head that I felt at all safe around. A lot of the Heads looked tough but were just goofballs. Chris was actually on the danger-ous side. He used to be on my bus and would talk about spending the night in jail and things like that. And since he was constantly suspended from school, I didn't have the opportunity to charm him in Gym class like I did a lot of the other Heads. So basically I was on the edge of wetting my pants. I thought maybe I could just say, "Mind if I 'play through'?" and go about my business, but that wasn't going to happen.

"Hey, Miracle Wimp," he said as I was weighing my escape plans.

"Uh, yes?"

"Where you going?"

"The health club?" I was so scared it sounded like a question.

He looked me up and down through bloodshot eyes.

"Get big, man."

"Okay," I said, and scurried off.

I have now
GOTTEN
BIG

Teacher Pants, Part II

So Trig was a real mix of people. Some of the students were underclassmen who were more advanced, but then there were also a few seniors who weren't quite as mathematically advanced as the others. Of course, as the year was winding down, the seniors were getting ready to be done with school early. They got out three weeks before everyone else to prepare for graduation. Because it's really hard to walk into an auditorium and sit down, or something. But they had one day left before they went, and they weren't missing any opportunities to rub it in. When it came to The Thing Beneath The Polyester, nothing was different. A note slowly made its way around the room, followed by stifled giggles. Mr. Grundie, as always, remained oblivious. It finally reached me. "Today is the last day we have to look at Mr. Grundie's business," it said, then added, "Chris says it's yucky today." Barely able to contain my laughter, I sent the note along.

Snap

Of course, Robert Manly had to snap eventually. You can't go on taking that sort of abuse on a regular basis and not have some anger built up.

Robert sat in front of me in Math. I never bothered him in regular classes. But this Donkey Joe did. Constantly. If it snowed, Joe would go to the windowsill, scoop up snow, and dump it down Robert's back. If he need to start over on his homework, he'd crumple up a piece of paper and throw it at Robert. And if he ever had to go hand something in at the teacher's desk, he'd be sure to bump Robert's head with his elbow as he walked past.

Turns out this was a bad habit. One day, which seemed like any other, Joe walked up to hand in some classwork while Mr. Grundie was up at the blackboard writing out the homework assignment. He turned around to walk back to his seat, and as he passed Robert, Robert's arm shot straight up, so quickly it seemed like it didn't even happen, and nailed Joe in the nose with a loud crack. Blood came rushing out, and Joe's eyes began to water, but he was so shocked that he just went and sat down in his seat like nothing had happened. He pulled some tissue from his pocket, which did little to stop the torrent of blood, and nothing to stop the tears. Robert had turned in his chair, facing Joe, his face crimson, waiting for Joe to say something that would give him an excuse to get up and finish the job. But Joe just sat there.

Finally Mr. Grundie turned around and seemed confused about why everyone was looking at Robert and Joe. Then he saw the bloody nose and the red face and realized what happened.

"Alright, you two, down to the office."

"Uh, Mr. Grundie," I said, "I really don't think it's a good idea to send them out into the hall together."

Mr. Grundie looked annoyed at my challenging his edict, but realized I was right.

"Joe, you go to the nurse and have her call us when you get there."

Later on, at lunch, the Goon Squad decided it was no longer a good idea to pick on Robert.

Goon Squad Induction

Since Robert had proven himself to be so dangerous, not only did we decide to not pick on him, but we decided to let him into the Goon Squad. He certainly had more fighting skills than the rest of us.

The obvious choice for his title would have been Sergeant-at-Arms or Hitman or something, but Robert insisted on "Nose Cracka."

We weren't going to argue with him.

NOSE CRACKA!

Bombs Away

Robert really wanted to do something wild in celebration of his triumph. He told us this one day in lunch. Steve and I had just come in, and Robert was getting ready to leave.

"I've got a smoke bomb and I want to set it off in school somewhere," he said. I think he was feeling a little invincible.

"Where?" I asked. It seemed like kind of a hard thing to hide doing.

"I don't know, and I've got to get back to class."

We thought about it.

"Light it, and drop it in the trash as you walk out," Steve said.

This seemed like a good plan.

We watched as Robert walked up to the trash, trying to act casual while looking around for teachers and trying to get his matches ready. Right when he got to the trash, Mr. Hammo happened to walk right in the cafeteria door next to him. This was not good at all. Robert looked at us. We shrugged. He stuffed everything into his pockets and stormed out of the cafeteria.

Mission Accomplished

When the fire alarm went off not ten minutes after Robert left the lunchroom, we knew he had to be behind it.

As we sat on the grass outside the cafeteria for the next hour and a half, we wanted to figure out what he had done, but couldn't say anything to anyone for fear of giving him away.

The Assembly

When we were finally allowed back into the school building, we all had to meet for an emergency assembly in the auditorium. Mr. Hammo walked up to the microphone and tapped it a few times. "May I have your attention, please?"

The buzz kept going. Everyone was too wound up to pay attention to him right now.

"May I have your attention, please?" he said a little louder.

Everyone still kept chattering.

"I thought I was talking to a group of high school students!" Mr. Hammo shouted.

Everyone stopped talking, and in unison, as if rehearsed, said, "Ooooooh!"

I love that sort of thing.

The Perfect Crime

The gist of the assembly was that they thought some smoker had thrown a cigarette butt into an abandoned locker that happened to be full of paper, which of course caught on fire. They were right about the abandoned locker anyway. They'd never suspect Robert, even if they somehow found out a smoke bomb had caused this. The perfect crime. He was late to class anyway, so while he was alone in the hall, he tossed the bomb into that locker, forgetting that there were papers inside, and when those got hot enough, the Vinnie's Magic Funk must have gone up. That's why we were out there for so long. A Magic Funk fire doesn't go down easily.

The Asking Out

"Hi, Heather? This is Tom Mayo, from the TV show thing at Abby's house."

"Hello, Tom."

"Hi. How are you?"

She giggles. "I'm fine. And you?"

"I'm good. I'm pretty good."

"That's good."

"Yes, it is. So, you're probably wondering why I'm calling."

"People do usually have a reason."

"Yeah, I guess they do. Well, I wanted to see if you wanted to go to Northampton some time this weekend. Some night maybe."

"That sounds like it might be fun."

"Well, which night is better for you?"

"Which night is better for *you*?"

"I'm free both nights."

"Well, let me check my schedule. Hmm. I also seem to be free both nights. What a coincidence."

"Yeah, that is odd. How about Saturday, then?"

"Ah, making me wait the extra day."

"Well, I just thought Friday, with school and all . . ."

"Relax, I'm just giving you a hard time."

"Oh."

"And anyway, Saturday night is traditionally date night."

"Okay, then. Should I pick you up at seven?"

"Seven is good."

"I'll see you then."

"Bye."

"Bye."

Let's go to work!

Aw Crap

Of course, in spite of all my planning to get all the details of the actual date out of her, I neglected to find out her address, and had to make a second, more embarrassing call.

Planning

I am so not sure of what to do now. Maybe I ought to just wear my wampum belt, and it'll all be smooth sailing.

The Nerd Hierarchy Revisited

Now that we're friends with Robert, I kind of realized I'm no better than Rob and Barry. Why did I pick on Robert? Or anyone? I mean, Rob and Barry were jerks to Larry because they wanted to be cool. I don't even want to be cool. So maybe that makes me an even bigger jerk.

Freak

You know, on the one hand, you have the fact that Mr. Boort is kind of a freak. Honestly. Sure, it's entertaining, but the guy is undeniably out there.

On the other hand, that's kind of cool. He totally doesn't care that he's a freak. He operates in his own little world. Which I suppose is kind of delusional, but still pretty cool. I try to ignore what most people think too, but it's not always that easy. I guess Mr. Boort has more practice than I do, since he's been at it longer. Given a choice between a Mr. Boort and a Mr. Zerot, it's no contest.

Wax Lips

So Heather and I hit Northampton. It didn't take long to run out of book and record stores to go into, so we started to go into the stores that were only sort of interesting, in the same way farm league baseball is. Not so hot, but you'll take what you can get. After viewing a lot of overpriced housewares, the next store we passed was a candy store. Huge "no sampling" signs were posted on all the bins of candy, and the place was small enough that they'd probably catch you if you tried. I was eyeing the Swedish fish anyway, waiting to see if the clerk would turn his back just long enough.

"Hey, wax lips," I heard Heather say.

I walked over to where she was. "Do you want red or black?" she said.

I looked at the ridiculously large blobs of colored paraffin. "I think red goes better with my skin tone," I said.

She handed the clerk a dollar and then she handed me the lips and we walked out without waiting for a receipt.

"Let's see if they work," I said, opening the plastic package and stuffing it in my pocket. I put the lips in and bit into the wax just enough to keep them from falling out.

"You look FABulous," she said. She made a kissy noise with her lips at me. Did the wax lips block the kiss from getting to me?

We walked along not saying much because it was hard to talk with the lips in. But I thought it was cool that we could be quiet together. Some people think they need to be talking all the time, but sometimes it gets annoying. I liked the quiet.

A group of people walked by and then from behind us I heard one of them yell, "Wax lips! Wax lips!" Then this excited little guy with a perm and a moustache came running up to me.

"Where'd you get the wax lips?"

I pointed down the street. "The candy shop on the corner," Heather said.

"Wax lips!" the guy shouted as he ran back to his friends to drag them to the candy store.

We sat down on the curb. A little guy who looked like Santa came stumbling towards us. We looked up at him. He looked at me with the lips and mumbled, "Goddamn kids on junk," and continued staggering down the street.

The End of the Evening

Heather and I walked out of the house, down the driveway to my car. We both stood there, not really sure of what was supposed to happen at that point.

"I guess I'll call you tomorrow," I said.

"Okay," she said.

Then we stood there looking at each other.

"I guess Abby has a bet with Gilbert that we won't kiss each other good night," Heather finally said.

"Oh," I said, not really knowing what to say about that.

"Do you want to make her lose?"

We Are Now Going to Work

This was good. This was very good.

In fact, this might very well have been awesome.

Awesome indeed.

Maybe Larry messed around in the computer and made some changes for me.

I mean, if that's how it works.

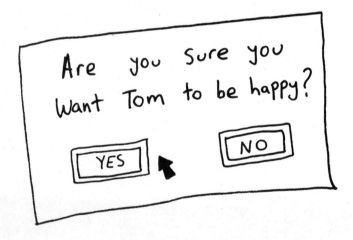

That Monday

Everything is better when you like someone. I mean, school is still full of dinks and everything, but somehow it's not as bad. I guess because I'm too busy obsessing about Heather to obsess about what brainless comment someone will make to me next, or what Rob and Barry are going to put in my senior activities in two years, or whether or not there are crabs in the pool.

Why can't I feel like this all the time?

There They Go

I really have to hand it to the Donkeys sometimes. They find new and unusual ways to torment, despite their limited brain capacities.

"Yo, Miracle Wimp, I heard you got a girlfriend in another town."

"Uh, yeah, sure."

"Pfft. Yeah, what town, CANADA?"

"Canada's a country, not a town."

"Hey, up yours, college boy!"

Baseball

With late spring came baseball. With baseball came "around the horn." After every out I felt compelled to yell, "around the horn!" and then the infield has to throw the ball around the bases. It was usually only funny for the first inning of the first game of the season, but I would try to keep it going for as long as I could. Sometimes, if I could keep it going long enough, it would get funny all over again, just for the ridiculousness of it all. And sometimes it would be a good time just because people would get so annoyed. "Around the horn!"

"Mayo, cut the shit."

"Mayo cuts the shit, leaving the pitcher headless!"

They thought they could stop me by putting me in the outfield, but they were wrong. I can yell "around the horn" anywhere they put me.

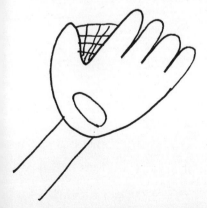

The Day I Got a Detention with Mr. Boort

Man. Detention in Wood Shop. That's the pits. All the crap that goes on, and I'm the one who gets in trouble. Amazing. Especially when all I did was hold the blade of my loom and and scream, "I'll cut you so BAD!" at Robert. I guess Mr. Boort was having a bad day or something. Maybe he didn't know Robert and I were friends now.

So, 2:10. I arrived in Shop. Mr. Boort wasn't around, so I just sat in the room where attendance is taken. No "let's go to work" today. After a little while, Mr. Boort wandered in with a cup of coffee. He came in the room, looked at me, grunted, "Mayo," then sat at his desk. He started doing the crossword. I sat there nervously. "Am I supposed to do anything?" I asked after a little while.

"No, just sit there," he said.

After about five minutes of awkward silence, he finally said, "Why are you in this class anyway?"

"Um," I said. "They messed up my schedule and wouldn't fix it."

"Mr. Banke?" he said. He smirked. "Are you at least getting anything out of being here?"

"Well," I said, starting to get uncomfortable, "it's okay, I guess. I suppose I'd like it more if we got to pick our own projects to work on."

"You know what would happen if I let you kids make whatever you wanted? I'd have a room full of dead kids. You think I don't notice what you get up to out there?"

What was I supposed to say to that?

"I know these projects are ridiculous. I plan it that way so people stay busy. I know hearts in a magazine rack are dumb, but it takes time. That keeps everyone busy, and that's all I'm here for. They don't care if I teach anything so long as I keep the idiots under control."

"Why do you do this if you don't like it?"

"Gotta put food on the table," he said. "I've done worse things." He pointed to a tattoo on his forearm that said "Korea— Never Forget."

"Well, what would you do if you could do anything?" I asked.

"I used to be a cabinetmaker," he said. "I enjoyed that. But no one wants to pay for things that are well made any- more. So here I am."

"You don't think you were meant to be a shop teacher?"

"You think you're some kind of comedian or something?"

"Er, no," I said. "Just, you know, how some people think people are destined to do certain things."

"That's something bolos say to make themselves feel

better about their crappy lives. Or to get out of having to work hard." He started to work on the crossword again. "Anyway, if you want to act like a peanuthead, that's your business. Otherwise, you seem like an okay kid. If you want to make up your own project to work on, I suppose I can let you do that, seeing as how it's not your fault you're here."

Dance Party

One of Heather's favorite TV shows was a public access show called "Boogietown Dance Party." It was basically a bunch of middle-aged people dancing to the latest radio hits in their wood-paneled basement. There were Christmas lights hung up, the ladies had big hair, and all the men had moustaches. It was pretty incredible.

"A few of these people are the parents of kids at our school," Heather said. "Their poor, poor children," she'd say whenever they were really getting down.

But Boogietown Dance Party was more than just quality entertainment. Every once in a while, Heather and her friends would pick out a place in Northampton that was having bands play, show up, and take everyone to Boogietown. They only did it if they had enough people for a "safety in numbers" effect, and they usually only did it for twenty minutes or so, and then escaped before an angry mob chased them out. Pretty cool.

"Do you ever do it at school dances?" I asked.

"Oh God, no," she said. "The point is to do it to people we'll never see again. I can't imagine how badly we'd get harassed if we did it at school. No sense in giving them more ammunition."

Long Drive

Now that I have my license and a girl who likes me, I get to drive a half hour to her house every Friday and Saturday night. And what do we do? We drive around or watch TV. Is this better than just staying at home and watching TV with Steve and Adam? I guess to other people, sometimes the fact that you have a girlfriend makes you cooler somehow. That's how I used to look at it. I'm not sure why. Aside from the kissing, this isn't all that different from my regular friends, save for the distance. Well, I guess it is a little more exciting, but the excitement is beginning to wear off.

Northampton

So, if I was lucky, I could convince Heather to go to Northampton when I was out visiting. But even someplace fun can get boring if you go there all the time. Plus, two nights in a row was too much. And even when we went and had fun, it was kind of a tease, since what little money I was making was spent on gas getting out to her house. Going to cool record/book/trinket stores is no fun if you can't buy anything.

Sometimes we'd go over to her friends' houses, but we'd really just watch TV there too. I mean, they all had the deluxe cable, which was way more than I had, but it still got boring. Sometimes we'd all listen to music and they'd talk about stuff that went on in their school. It was kind of interesting to hear about how things went for them, but it usually just boiled down to them complaining about how many girls liked Gilbert, and how Gilbert wasn't interested in any of them, but a lot of guys wanted to beat him up because of it anyway. They also talked a lot about how school was "heavy."

They seemed really cool and interesting the night we made the video.

"Heavy"

Heather and her friends think a lot of stuff is heavy.

School, obviously.

Parents. Their town.

Driving is a big one. Heather is totally old enough to drive, but doesn't have her license because the driver's test is heavy, and traffic is usually heavy too.

All this heaviness is crushing me.

See?

"Are you coming over this weekend?" she asked me.

"Sure. Are we doing anything?"

"I don't know. We'll figure it out when you get here."

"Okay," I said. "Well, I mean, it's really nice out. We should do something outside instead of just watching TV."

"Sorry if I'm not exciting enough for you."

"That's not what I meant."

"Then what did you mean?"

"I don't know, it's just . . ." I stopped for a minute, not wanting it to come out wrong. "I have to drive a long way to get to your house, so I just want to do something fun."

"Spending time with me isn't fun?"

"That's not what I said. We just always watch TV lately."

"Don't come over if you don't want to see me."

"Look, that's not it. Don't worry about it, I'll be there."

TV

When I hung out with Steve and Adam, I could draw when we watched TV and it was no big deal. If I tried to draw when I watched TV with Heather, it was big trouble.

"Why don't you just stay home if that's what you want to do?"

"We're just watching TV."

"You're not even paying attention to me."

"You're watching TV, you're not really paying attention to me either."

"It's different."

"How so?"

"It just is. Stop drawing or go home."

Not Impressed

Heather was also not so impressed with my jeans.

"Where the hell did you get those awful things?"

"The 99-cent store."

"You paid 99 cents for those?"

"No, they've changed their policy about the 99-cent thing."

"Well, don't wear those ever again."

"It's just a joke, really. Mr. Boort wears them."

"I don't want to go out with Mr. Boort."

"They're just pants. I mean, oh forget it."

Decisions, Decisions

I'm not sure what to do, really. Is being with a girlfriend who is kind of a drag better than being with no girlfriend at all? I wasn't expecting this.

Sometimes I think "at least I have a girlfriend," but then I think about Larry, and if I died unexpectedly, do I want to be unhappy when it happens? But what would make me unhappier?

I wonder what Mr. Banke would suggest I do. Ha! Then again, a Magic 8 Ball would give just as reliable advice.

Anyone know where I can get one of those things?

Breakup

"So are you coming out this weekend?" Heather asked me, as happened every Thursday.

Except this time, I wasn't really sure what to say.

"I guess so," I said after a probably too-long pause.

"Don't do me any favors," she said.

I took a deep breath.

"Look," I said. "I don't think I can go on like this. I think we should maybe . . ." I wasn't sure how to put it, and I was starting to well up, and I didn't want to cry on the phone.

"Take a break?" she said after a really long pause.

"Yeah," I said.

More silence.

"Okay," she said.

"Yeah," I said.

"But do you still want to come hang out this weekend?" she asked.

"Yeah, okay, I'll do that," I said.

I didn't really have anything else to do. You know, except sit around and wonder if I had done the right thing.

Support

It was one of those phone pickups where you hear the phone get picked up, but something is in the middle of going on, and they're going to finish it before they get to you.

"Look, I said we'd go, just let me answer the phone already," I heard Adam say. "Hello?"

"Hey," I said. "It's Tom." I started welling up again. "I . . . I just broke up with Heather."

"Oh shit," he said. Then I heard Becky Frunecki saying something in the background. "Hang on," he said. I think he put his hand over the phone, because I could hear arguing, but I couldn't make out what was being said.

"Look, man," Adam finally said, "I'm really sorry, I have to go. I'll talk to you later, maybe?"

"Yeah, sure," I said.

Later

Post-Breakup Hangout

So I went out to see Heather that weekend. Not only was I worried about hanging out, but then it occurred to me that her mother might also be around, and what if she knew we broke up? That would make it extra awful, if awful was the direction it was going to go in. Luckily, her mother was almost never around.

The plus side of having just broken up was that she was much more receptive to doing stuff other than watching TV.

The downside was that we weren't going out anymore.

But I got there, and we were going to go to Northampton. And it was a little weird. She just said, "Hi," and let me in, and went to get her shoes because she wasn't ready. She sat on the couch, and as she was putting them on, the sun was shining in through the window behind her. I couldn't even really see her face because of the light being behind her, but something about it made her look extra cute, and it just kept me wondering if I had done the right thing.

Confusion

Is it normal to keep hanging out with someone all the time after you've broken up with them? It was kind of like going out still, just less hand holding and kissing. And she was much more receptive to letting me draw during TV, if we even ended up watching TV at all. But it felt weird and not weird at the same time. I mean, it was not weird because we liked each other obviously, but if we weren't "going out," why were we spending so much time together?

The Junior Prom

So Heather and I were supposed to go to the junior prom to-gether. I guess we still were. Was that going to be weird? Prob-ably. I didn't know. Having never gone out with someone be-fore her, I'd obviously never broken up with anyone, either. The protocol eluded me. Would we go and pretend like we were still going out? Or would it be really awkward? A little of both? Probably. I mean, we'd already paid for the tickets, so I didn't want to be out that money. I guess we'd just go through with it and see what'd happen.

Junior Prom Night

In spite of my vast riches from the health
club, I could not afford a limo for the
prom. That was o.k. Taking a
limo to the prom is kind
of a Donkey thing any-
way. Plus, having the
limo drive all the way
out to Heather's and
back would probably
have made it really expensive. So I just drove us. Not
so flashy, but what are you
going to do?

   I did get the ugliest plaid tuxedo I could find, and Heather
got this silver sparkly dress that seemed to be a reject from
the disco era. Sure, we were going to a "normal" high school
event, but we were going to "make it sing."

Hoedown

You know what? The prom is really, really boring. Or at least the junior prom. I doubt the senior prom is any different, and I think I understand why so many people get drunk beforehand. Snore city. You get a decent meal, but then you just sit around listening to music you don't like, watching people you don't like dance drunkenly.

"This thing shits," I said.

"Yeah," Heather agreed.

I looked out at the idiots.

"You know," I said, "I think this event would be complemented nicely by a touch of Boogietown Dance Party."

She giggled. "Are you serious?"

"I have never felt so strongly about something in my life," I said, and I took her by the hand, and we walked to the dance floor.

Lord and Lady of the Dance

We really outdid ourselves. My tux had nary a breathable fiber in it, so I got authentically sweaty for the Boogietown effect. We pulled out all the stops, move-wise. I spun her around, I dipped her, we shimmied at each other while squatting up and down, all of it. If anyone had been taking pictures, they could have used them to illustrate a Boogietown Dance Party instructional book.

It was kind of a blast. We really had a hard time not cracking up. It's very important for authenticity to look as serious as possible. When we'd exhausted our repertoire of moves and went back to our table, so many people actually came by and *complimented* us.

"Tom, man, you guys can really *dance*! I had no idea! Awesome!"

BOOGIETOWN
The Book!
(giant bangs sold seperately)

Learn to dance like an idiot!

Drop-off

I was pretty tired out from all the dancing and sweating, and then I had to drive Heather home.

"Did you want to go to any of the after-parties?" I asked.

"Not really," she said. "I think after the dancing, anything else would be a letdown."

"Yeah," I said. "That was pretty amazing."

"I had a really good time tonight," she said.

"Yeah, I did too," I said. "I never expected the prom to be that much fun."

Was I supposed to kiss her good night? I felt like I wanted to.

"Well, good night," she said. She leaned in to kiss me. I went for her cheek, figuring that was a good compromise, but she got me right on the lips. A quick one, but on the lips nonetheless.

Coming at you...

The End

So I don't know what's going on. If Larry's up there messing around with the cosmic computer, he either doesn't know what he's doing, or he found solitaire or some porn or something. Maybe this whole cosmic computer thing is a stupid idea. If it is, does that make me a bolo?

Everyone is somebody's bolo.

Aren't they?